S0-APO-908

An Old Scandal

by

Caroline Brooks

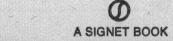

A SIGNET BOOK

NEW AMERICAN LIBRARY

NAL BOOKS ARE AVAILABLE AT QUANTITY DISCOUNTS WHEN USED TO
PROMOTE PRODUCTS OR SERVICES. FOR INFORMATION PLEASE WRITE
TO PREMIUM MARKETING DIVISION, NEW AMERICAN LIBRARY, 1633
BROADWAY, NEW YORK, NEW YORK 10019.

Copyright © 1985 by Caroline Brooks

All rights reserved

SIGNET TRADEMARK REG. U.S. PAT. OFF. AND FOREIGN COUNTRIES
REGISTERED TRADEMARK—MARCA REGISTRADA
HECHO EN CHICAGO, U.S.A.

SIGNET, SIGNET CLASSIC, MENTOR, PLUME, MERIDIAN
and NAL BOOKS are published by New American Library,
1633 Broadway, New York, New York 10019

First Printing, April, 1985

1 2 3 4 5 6 7 8 9

PRINTED IN THE UNITED STATES OF AMERICA

Good +8

This was the sweetest loneliest love
story two people who to ~~meet~~ across
time and space take one well

UNMASKING UMBERTO

Leonora should have been grateful to have
had her worst fears and darkest suspicions
about Lord Umberto confirmed in time to save
her from surrendering to him.

She should have blessed the moment when at
the masquerade ball she spied Umberto,
dressed as a gypsy, intimately embracing the
Russian Princess Bagration, dressed in virtually
nothing at all. But why then did Leonora's
new-won wisdom of the world feel more
painful than her former folly of falling in love
with this maddeningly attractive but hopelessly
infamous lord who lied as easily as he laughed?
And how could she force herself to halt the
absurd rebellion of her own traitor heart . . . ?

At each other and fall in love
Wonderful cute ending
deserving

An Old Scandal

10

BOOKMARK

2073 N. WEST
WICHITA KS
67203

More Delightful Regency Romances from SIGNET

		(0451)
☐	THE ACCESSIBLE AUNT by Vanessa Gray.	(126777—$2.25)
☐	THE DUKE'S MESSENGER by Vanessa Gray.	(118685—$2.25)*
☐	THE DUTIFUL DAUGHTER by Vanessa Gray.	(090179—$1.75)*
☐	RED JACK'S DAUGHTER by Edith Layton.	(129148—$2.25)*
☐	THE MYSTERIOUS HEIR by Edith Layton.	(126793—$2.25)
☐	THE DISDAINFUL MARQUIS by Edith Layton.	(124480—$2.25)*
☐	THE DUKE'S WAGER by Edith Layton.	(120671—$2.25)*
☐	A SUITABLE MATCH by Joy Freeman.	(117735—$2.25)*
☐	THE NOBLE IMPOSTER by Mollie Ashton.	(129156—$2.25)*

*Prices slightly higher in Canada

Buy them at your local bookstore or use this convenient coupon for ordering.

NEW AMERICAN LIBRARY,
P.O. Box 999, Bergenfield, New Jersey 07621

Please send me the books I have checked above. I am enclosing $＿＿＿＿＿
(please add $1.00 to this order to cover postage and handling). Send check
or money order—no cash or C.O.D.'s. Prices and numbers are subject to change
without notice.

Name ＿＿＿＿＿＿＿＿＿＿＿＿＿＿＿＿＿＿＿＿＿＿＿＿＿＿＿＿＿＿

Address＿＿＿＿＿＿＿＿＿＿＿＿＿＿＿＿＿＿＿＿＿＿＿＿＿＿＿＿

City＿＿＿＿＿＿＿＿＿＿ State＿＿＿＿＿＿ Zip Code＿＿＿＿＿＿
Allow 4-6 weeks for delivery.
This offer is subject to withdrawal without notice.

1

THE FINE MISTY autumn rain, which had been threatening to fall all that day, had finally broken from the clouds in a steady downpour that trickled down the panes of the common-room windows like teardrops from heaven.

But neither the proprietor of Les Trois Poissons nor the young person with whom he was engaged in a spirited dialogue noted this change in the weather, so intent were they upon their loud and spirited disagreement. The landlord's English was as limited as the young person's French, and so, perhaps it was inevitable that what had started in low and civilized tones should rapidly be reaching the pitch of hysteria that brought the chambermaids from their duties to lean, wide-eyed, over the stairs.

The young person twisted the ribbons of her chipstraw bonnet between her fingers and shook her head; the landlord waved his arms about in the air but neither seemed to be able to budge an inch upon their separately held theories that if one spoke one's native language clearly and distinctly, anyone should be able to comprehend what was being said, with the consequence that the young person's English became progressively more disjointed, and the landlord's French increasingly threatening, until the only person in the Calais inn not aware of this interesting scene seemed to be the dark gentleman in the taproom, who appeared to find a bottle of fine old *ancien régime* brandy worthy of his full attentions.

"If you would only be good enough to send to Paris, to Lord and Lady Somerville, I assure you that they will straighten this affair out instantly," the young person was repeating for perhaps the twentieth time to the uncomprehending proprietor, when the glass doors on Les Trois Poissons swung back on their hinges.

The entrance of the woman who swept through those doors was enough to silence both the young person and the landlord.

From the quivering green plumes in her Récamier bonnet to the tips of her orange jean half-boots, she was unmistakably an English lady of fashion. Lifting her quizzing glass to her eye, she surveyed, without any particular interest, the young person, the landlord, the furnishings of the room, and the dark gentleman in the tap, who seemed to have finally found a subject more diverting than brandy, for he was in the process of raising his own glass to his eye when the lady allowed hers to drop and turned away.

Her unexpected appearance thus was enough to take the landlord away from his dialogue with the young person, for while clean and respectable, Les Trois Poissons was hardly the sort of establishment that attracted the rich *anglaises* who had been attacking Calais in hordes since the recent peace. But who could blame that man if, with good Gallic logic, he assumed that the lady of fashion and the young person, both being English, were in some way connected, and advanced upon the lady with a violent torrent of French?

Lady Leonora Ware, whose command of French was, at best, rather limited, watched the landlord advancing on her for only a split second before lifting her glass again; after all, the sight of one gray eye, hideously magnified, should have been enough to depress the pretensions of the most encroaching individual.

But the landlord was a republican and not to be dissuaded from his purpose, no doubt in the fervent belief that he was making all clear as day.

"Really, sir," Lady Leonora drawled, making a dismissive gesture with her reticule in this person's direction. "I have not the slightest interest in your family quarrels, so if you would be so good as to provide me with a private parlor and a glass of Madeira—"

"This man is no relation to *me*, ma'am!" exclaimed the young person in accents so indignant and so English that in spite of herself, Lady Leonora was forced to study her more closely.

"Bath miss" was writ large upon the young

person, from the pink ribbons decorating her chipstraw hat to the ruched hem of her sadly rumpled spring muslin, peering out from beneath a drab pelisse. Clusters of guinea-gold curls framed a face uniquely English and at the moment stained with two bright spots of color in either cheek. A pair of blue eyes met Leonora's quizzical gaze defiantly, but beneath, it was easy to see that tears were about to start flowing at any second. "Runaway" was the word that formed in Leonora's mind, and a tiny warning signal triggered itself in her head. But it had long been Lady Leonora Ware's policy to never inconvenience herself in the affairs of others, and she was about to turn away when the girl allowed a single tear to roll down her cheek.

"Oh, here now! Pray, do not become a watering pot! It would be a dead bore, you know, and I cannot abide dead bores," Lady Leonora said rather gruffly, concealing her distress by rooting about in her reticule for a handkerchief.

As she was doing this, she heard the unmistakable sound of a smothered chuckle coming from the direction of the tap, and, from a corner of her eye, caught a glimpse of the dark English gentleman enjoying the scene enormously.

It was this, more than the Bath miss's tears, that decided Lady Leonora upon the unprecedented course of taking charge of the situation, much against her better judgment and inclination. But there was no one present who could know Leonora Ware's reputation for never putting herself forward when her own comfort was in question.

Several years as a young and comfortable widow had left Leonora well-versed in depressing the pretensions of a person such as the dark gentleman, and with a practiced ease she lifted her quizzing glass again to take in every detail of his person, from his gleaming boots to his elegantly tied cravat. Seemingly not at all discomfited, the gentleman bowed in his seat. He was, Leonora noted, disconcertingly handsome—if one liked dark and craggy men, of course, which she did not. With a haughty sniff, she turned away from him, only to find that the landlord had caught his second wind and was again launching into a voluble diatribe, of which she understood perhaps every tenth word.

With a flounce of her sables, Lady Leonora stared him down also, leaving his opinions of the amount of freedom given to young English ladies and of the state of moral decay in the world at large to trail away into silence.

Satisfied that she held the floor, Lady Leonora turned her attention toward the Bath miss again, tendering her a handkerchief, which was gratefully accepted.

"Now, if you please, precisely what is happening here?" Lady Leonora asked, not unkindly, as the Bath miss blew her nose.

"Th-thank you, ma'am! I do not know what I would have done if you had not rescued me! I seem to have embroiled myself in quite the most ridiculous tangle, and this man simply won't understand! If you would only be good enough to explain to him that I didn't know that I did not have enough to pay for my dinner—travel

is so expensive, far more than I had imagined—
and if he would send to L-Lord and Lady
Somerville in Paris, I know that they will send
me some money!" She opened her eyes very
wide at Lady Leonora as if she believed that my
lady were capable of solving any problem.

A not entirely unflattered Lady Leonora put
a gloved hand upon the shoulder of the Bath
miss. "Here now! I am certain that we may
straighten this all out! Money! It always does
seem to come to money, does it not? But where
is your guardian, child? Young ladies do not
make their way into France alone!"

"This one did!" the Bath miss said very
proudly.

"A thousand pardons, madame, but there is
not another inn in Calais that is not full to the
rafters!"

All of them turned toward the door, and
for the moment, Leonora, the dark gentleman,
the Bath miss, and the landlord all forgot their
altercation as a vision in lemon-yellow panta-
loons, a plum traveling cloak, and ornately po-
maded hair stepped briskly through the doorway
on high-heeled boots, pressing a scented handkerchief against a pencil-thin mustache.

"Oh, René! Thank God you are here!" said
Lady Leonora, who had long ago become inured
to the effect her majordomo had upon other
people.

René raised one eyebrow as he tripped
delicately across the floor, looking about himself
with Gallic distaste.

René D'Aubusson, scion of a noble and

unfortunately extinct French family, had been with Leonora since the early days of her marriage. As a penniless émigré coming into the service of the late Lord Richard Ware, he had found a thousand ways of relieving his employers from the mundane chores of day-to-day living, and for this received an exorbitant salary that Leonora considered he was not earning at the moment by simply standing there.

Instead he was looking at his plum-colored greatcoat in distress, shaking his head. "The rain!" he lamented. "It has ruined the nap of this superfine!"

The dark gentleman in the tap, regarding René through the bottom of his glass, made a choking sound and reached for the brandy bottle again.

"René!" Lady Leonora said in her most imperious tones, and with a sigh of regret he folded the greatcoat over his arm and addressed the landlord as to the possibility of rooms for himself and his employer.

The landlord, finding himself thus addressed in his native tongue, could restrain himself no longer, and with words and gestures, poured out a torrent upon the hapless René that made that person take a step backward and press his handkerchief against his mustache once again.

Lady Leonora sighed, feeling the ennui creeping up on her. "Just ask him how much he wants, René, and have done," she murmured.

"Pardon, madame, but he seems to be under the misapprehension that the young lady is a part of our party." René was clearly amused at the very thought. "He says that we must pay for her nuncheon of ham, veal, cheese, bread tarts, and fruit before we may go any further."

"I was hungry," the Bath miss said apologetically. "I hadn't eaten since we left Dover."

"He further states," René continued, eyeing the Bath miss doubtfully, "that the English have a great deal to answer for in allowing their young girls so much freedom. Such a thing would never be allowed in France."

There was a strangled sound from the tap, and Lady Leonora turned to give the dark gentleman a speaking look, only to find him displaying an inordinate interest in his brandy glass.

René took a deep breath. "Madame, he further states that Les Trois Poissons is a respectable inn, although it may not be in the first style of fashion, and furthermore, he is not in the habit of allowing penniless and unescorted schoolgirls, whom he strongly suspects of having run away from their schools, as guests—"

"If I must hear another thing that this person thinks," Lady Leonora announced firmly, "I will scream."

"Pardon, madame," René intoned, looking up at the ceiling, "but the landlord also wishes to add that morals have declined immeasurably since the wars, and he deplores such conditions very deeply."

"You may ask him if he has a room for myself, a room for you, and a room for the Bath miss—I beg your pardon, my dear, I didn't catch your name," Leonora added quickly. "Since there is no other inn in Calais that is not filled to the rafters, and it is beginning to rain, I believe that we must make the best of this, although if this man insists upon prosing on, I will be reduced to strong hysterics, which are frequently quite effective."

The innkeeper, who had always suspected, with good reason, that the English were an uncivilized race, responded admirably to this member of the *ancien régime* now that there was a certainty that the Bath miss's bill would be settled. Although he privately dismissed the lot of them as deranged, he expressed the deepest desire to accommodate, but alas with the great number of *anglaises* flooding into Calais, there was only one room available. Even the maid had been put up on a trundle in order to accommodate more guests.

When this had been translated for Lady Leonora, she merely shook her head and began to draw off her gloves. "Here we are, here I mean to stay," she announced in the tones of one used to having her own way. "I am quite exhausted, and I refuse to take another step this night, if I have to sleep on a shakedown in the parlor." Suddenly her eye fell upon the dark gentleman in the tap, and an idea formed within her mind.

"You, sir." She beckoned imperiously.

The dark gentleman looked up warily, then all about himself in the empty room. Finally concluding that he was being addressed by the lady, he rose unsteadily to his feet. He was, Lady Leonora could not help but notice, very tall, very dark, and very handsome, and very *foxed*. "In what way may I serve you, ma'am?" he asked, swaying a little as he bowed in her direction, his crooked grin exposing a row of even white teeth. Under other circumstances, she might have forgiven a great deal for the sake of a pair of fine dark eyes, but now she was all pragmatism, as she crooked a finger in his direction.

"You, sir, are in possession of a room in this establishment?" she asked in her most dulcet tones.

The dark gentleman, perhaps sensing what was coming, swallowed and nodded warily.

"A single room?" she pursued sweetly.

Again the gentleman nodded. "But I—"

Sweeping aside all protests with one gloved hand, Lady Leonora smiled her most charming smile. Since she was quite pretty, the effect could be devastating. "Good! Then you will not mind sharing it for one night with M. le Comte D'Aubusson!"

The dark gentleman, eyeing M. le Comte doubtfully, would clearly like nothing less, and opened and closed his mouth several times, running a finger about the inside of his cravat. A rather crafty expression filled his face. "I snore in a most deplorably loud way," he suggested hopefully.

"If you please, madame!" René interjected. "Rather than share a room with this man, I should prefer to sleep in the stables!"

"Nonsense!" Lady Leonora returned. "I am quite unequal to imagining you, of all people, sleeping in a cow byre, René!" Having settled this matter to her own satisfaction, if no one else's, Lady Leonora held out her hand to the dark gentleman. "I am very obliged to you, sir," she said sweetly.

The dark gentleman made a low bow over her hand of such awkwardness that she was afraid he would lose his balance. "I cannot help but feel that you *are*, ma'am," he agreed fervently.

Two faints spots of color appeared in Leonora's cheeks.

With a wry look at René, who sniffed disdainfully, the dark gentleman repaired to his brandy with such a grin in Lady Leonora's direction that she almost brought her quizzing glass to her eye again, for she had a strong feeling that he was evaluating her figure in a way that no gentleman would dream of doing.

Collecting herself, Leonora bid René have the landlord escort herself and the Bath miss to the room they would share. Repairing from the lists a little more ruffled than she had expected, Leonora could at least content herself with the notion that she had contributed strongly to the dark gentleman's discomfort.

While the little room to which Lady Leonora and her young companion were taken was not in the first style of elegance to which Lady Leonora was accustomed, it was neat and tidy, with chintz curtains at the windows and sheets that were clean and fresh, as Lady Leonora was careful to ascertain before dismissing the landlord with a nod of her head.

"Oh, ma'am, you are such a perfect hand!"

the Bath miss exclaimed in admiring accents the moment the door was shut upon them.

"Yes, I suppose I am," Lady Leonora said complacently as she peered into the looking glass to undo the strings of her bonnet. "But when one has been upon the world as a widow as long as I have, one learns how to deal." Removing this frothy confection from her auburn curls, she turned to reveal herself as a female not more than ten years older than her companion, with a heart-shaped face, a pair of wide gray eyes, and a mouth both generous and slightly amused. It was a countenance somewhat incongruous with the languid and sophisticated air adopted by its owner, and the Bath miss had to blink once or twice to assure herself that this pretty young lady was indeed the fashionable female who had come to her rescue.

Oblivious of the wonderment of her companion, Lady Leonora placed her Récamier bonnet on the bureau and removed her pelisse, tossing it casually across the bed before sinking gratefully into a chair, putting her feet up, and regarding the Bath miss with a thoughtful expression. "Now, my dear," she began, "I think it best you and I have a comfortable coze. It does not do, you know, for you to be jaunting about the French countryside unescorted. People are likely to take you for an adventuress, and that would *hardly* do. One does not create scenes with innkeepers, you know, for sooner or later you are liable to get in above your head with no one to rescue you."

The Bath miss looked rather woebegone,

drawing off her chipstraw bonnet and her bedraggled pelisse. "But I was so hungry!" she exclaimed. "You see, ma'am, I thought I had enough money to get to Paris, but everything was so expensive—the passage from Dover was five pounds!—and so, when I came to Les Tres Poissons, because, you see, I thought it would be a place where no one would recognize me—"

"Ah! Traveling incognito, I assume?" Lady Leonora interjected, pulling off her gloves, finger by finger.

"Exactly so!" the Bath miss replied. "Oh, you do understand!"

"I understand nothing, my dear, so pray continue."

"Very well, then! It was only after I had eaten, and looked in my pocketbook to pay the shot, that I realized I had only a few shillings left. So I thought if the landlord could only be persuaded to send to my godparents in Paris, they would send me some money."

"Your godparents in Paris. Is that where you are trying to go?"

The Bath miss tried to look canny and failed. She was far too naive. "Not precisely," she admitted at last.

Lady Leonora sighed. In a rare moment of unselfishness, she had taken this poor girl under her wing, but now the idea of being saddled with a runaway barely out of the schoolroom was beginning to bore her profoundly. She decided that it behooved her to discover in what way she could soonest dispatch this reckless child back into the custody of her guardians, and with the least effort from herself. She had, after all, made this trip to the continent in search of a diversion from her restless boredom, not to become a bear leader for a runaway.

"Now, I think it would be best if you were to tell me the whole story," she said at last. "And no prevarications, mind you, for I warn you that I am not easily taken in."

The Bath miss regarded her for a moment with her chin thrust forward, a look Lady Leonora had no trouble in meeting with a calm gaze of her own. The Bath miss dropped her gaze, twisted her hands in her lap. "I am on my way to Vienna, to stay with my father!" she admitted.

"Ah! We make progress!" Leonora said. "Now, who is your father?"

"Sir Julian Hobart. He is attached to Lord Castlereagh's staff, for the peace negotiations, and if he had known what a perfectly dreadful place Miss Gunnerston's is, I am sure that he would never have sent me—"

"Miss Gunnerston's?" Leonora's air of languid boredom dropped away from her like a cloak and she sat bolt upright in her chair, her eyes flashing. "You have run away from Miss Gunnerston's in Bath?"

Miss Hobart looked quite terrified. She cowered in her chair. "Oh, if you please, ma'am, do not send me back! I would rather cast myself off the cliffs out there than go back to Bath!"

"I believe you!" Leonora retorted. "And so would I if I had to go back to that wretched, dreary, unhappy place!"

Miss Hobart's eyes grew very wide. "You did not—"

Leonora laughed. "Oh, yes, I did—and not so very many years ago, either! Do not tell me that old tabby is still running a school! It is unthinkable! How many times have I yearned to box her ears just once for all the times she boxed mine! Tell me, is she still there?"

"Oh, yes, and as odious as ever, I assure you!" Miss Hobart exclaimed.

"And her mustache?"

"Like a hussar's, only much more resplendent!" Miss Hobart assured her, and both of them went off in peals of laughter.

"So! You ran away from the Gunnerston shark!" Leonora said, her tone quite full of admiration. "How many times I yearned to do so, but always lacked the courage! You are to be congratulated."

"I doubt that Papa will think so," Miss Hobart murmured uncertainly. "But I do not think that he would have put me in there if he knew precisely how odious it would be." She turned a lock of guinea-gold hair around a finger. "Actually, I was to have made my come-out this season with my Cousin Eugenia, but Aunt Sophia has three spotty girls to launch, and I think she was reluctant to put me into the competition."

Lady Leonora, regarding Miss Hobart's blond and blue-eyed prettiness, could not help but feel sympathy for Aunt Sophia, but she held her tongue.

"So, you see, there being no other lady

suitable to bring me out, Papa had no other
solution but to put me into school. Mama died
right after I was born, and I had Miss Tiffingham,
my governess, until a couple of years ago, and
we went wherever Papa went, but now I am too
old for a governess so it was Miss Gunnerston's,
and ugh!"

"Well, my dear—you do have a name, do
you not?" Lady Leonora asked.

"Jane Elizabeth Hobart, ma'am."

"Very pretty! And I am Lady Leonora Ware,
if you please, although I was Leonora Samdrake
when I went to Miss Gunnerston's—"

"Oh!" Jane clapped her hands in delight.
"Your name is still where you carved it in the
commons hall!"

"Is it! Lord, I was on bread and water for a
fortnight for that prank!" Leonora laughed. "But
one of my brothers had sent me a penknife, and
I had to try it out!"

There was a knock upon the door, and René
thrust in his head, informing my lady that he
had arranged for a dinner to be served in a
private parlor.

"Well!" said Leonora, rising and shaking
some of the dust from her hem. "I am famished!
Travel is quite the thing to give one an appetite,
Sir Richard was always wont to say, and I declare
he was correct! But are you hungry, Jane? You
only ate a couple of hours ago . . ."

Leonora turned to look at her companion.
"Of course you are! Come along and eat something, and then we shall determine what we
should do with you!"

In very good accord, Lady Leonora and Miss Hobart descended a few moments later to the private parlor.

As was his custom, René had arranged everything to his employer's satisfaction. A fire burned cheerfully in the grate, and a fresh linen cloth had been spread across a table set for three and attended by a cheerful little maid in a starched cap and apron, who curtsied very deeply as the ladies entered the door.

René, who had long ago inured himself to Lady Leonora's restless whims, seated both ladies without so much as a tilt of the eyebrow at the presence of the Bath miss.

Indeed, he seemed to be entirely over his pique about the accommodations his employer had arranged for him, for René's temperament was sunny, and he was not inclined to hold a grudge overlong, even when Lady Leonora was at her most exasperating.

Over herbed chicken and an excellent white wine, René was quite ready to display a sympathetic interest in Jane's plight, dabbing at his lips with his napkin between bites of food and murmurs of *"Mon Dieu!* But how dreadful for you, miss! Do have just a splash more wine and a bit of this wonderful asparagus. . . ."

Lady Leonora, who was a fastidious eater, picked at her chicken and refilled her wineglass, watching in utter amazement as Jane Hobart, who had completed a late luncheon only a few hours before, did hearty justice to the dinner. Where, Leonora wondered, did the young put it all? If *she* ate like that, she would be the size of a house!

Just as Jane was reaching for her second piece of *gâteau aux fruits,* René revealed his inspiration. "I think that I may have a way out of Miss Hobart's troubles, madame!" he exclaimed, pouring Leonora a strong cup of coffee. "I think that we might take Miss Hobart up with us as far as Paris, since that is the direction in which we are headed. There, we may leave her with Lord and Lady Somerville, none the worse for her little adventure, *hein?*"

"An excellent suggestion, René," Lady Leonora said with relief. "For it would not do to leave you here, my dear, or to allow you to travel to Paris unescorted."

Jane smiled. "Oh, I should like above all things to travel with *you* to Paris, ma'am!" Her eyes sparkled, and it was clear that if René had suggested that they were traveling to the other side of the moon, she would have cheerfully accompanied them. Her admiration for Lady Leonora was writ large in her eyes.

Just at that moment, when her future was decided and her schoolgirl's appetite temporarily assuaged, Jane gave a large and startled yawn, which she quickly covered behind her hand. Her cheeks filled with rosy blushes and she exclaimed, "Oh! I am so sorry! I don't know what came over me!"

"*I* do!" Leonora laughed, putting her hand over Jane's. "You have had a very long and very tiring day, and now it is time for you to go to bed! So, say your good-nights, and off with you, for we rise very early in the morning!"

"Well, madame," said René when the door had closed behind Jane, after many thank-yous and good-nights, "it would appear that you have won an admiring schoolgirl."

Lady Leonora waved a languid hand. "Oh, pooh!" she said, but she was not entirely displeased. "You know that I think of no one but myself, René. Perhaps I think it would be amusing to while away a tedious journey with a lively companion."

René smiled, shaking his head. "Those who say that you have no heart, that you care only for fashionable amusements and society, do not know you as well as I." He examined his fingernails with great interest, a small smile playing about his lips.

"Ah, perhaps they know me better, René! Of course I have no heart! *Everyone* knows that!"

"Just as you wish, madame," René said complacently. He rose to his feet and placed his empty glass on the table. "And now, if you have no further need of me, madame, I shall retire to my chamber of horrors. I have no doubt that our friend in the tap will snore all the night through." He shuddered delicately and rolled his eyes so expressively that Lady Leonora was forced to laugh aloud.

"Admit, at least, that it is better than sleeping in a cow byre!" she teased him.

René merely bowed and wished her a good night as he took his leave, closing the door behind him.

Leonora settled back into her chair and withdrew a book from her reticule. Sleep was a thing that was in the habit of eluding her in strange places and climes, and she hoped that she might lull herself into the arms of Narcos with a novel some well-wisher had pressed upon her before her departure from London. The title, she thought, glancing at the spine, was unprepossessing: *Frankenstein; or the New Prometheus*. Nonetheless, she decided, it must be the perfect soporific, and cut the first page.

Two hours later, the fire was burning low on the grate, and the candle on the stand at her elbow was reduced to a mere stub, yet Leonora read on, wholly awake and utterly enthralled as Mrs. Shelley unfolded her terrible tale.

So engrossed in her book was Lady Leonora that she did not hear the door open, and when a shadow fell across the page, she gave a little shriek and threw the volume up in the air.

"Peace, I pray you, madam!"

The dark man stood above her, a finger to his lips, his expression most comical.

"Of all the odious things to do! How dare you, sir! *I* have bespoken this parlor!" She pointed a trembling finger toward the door. "Out at once, or I shall call down the house!"

The dark gentleman shook his head. "Peace! Peace, please! I beg of you! Trifle foxed! Thought there was no one in the room, but a nice warm fire that might be going still! Besides, I don't relish going up the stairs to share my room with your man-milliner there."

Leonora glared up at him. "You gave me a terrible start, sir!"

The dark gentleman, who had bent to retrieve Lady Leonora's book, read the title on the spine and grinned a crooked and oddly charming grin. "I am not surprised, if you chose to read this!" he replied, handing it back to her. "It kept me awake all one night! The hair stood upon my head the whole time, I assure you!"

Lady Leonora gave a little shiver. "Truly, sir! A most frightening story! When I saw you standing before me, I thought the monster had come!"

"Come now! I do not think that I am that wretched!" the dark gentleman replied, going to stand by the fire, where he warmed his hands in the glow of the embers.

"No—of course not!" Leonora replied quickly.

"I am most glad to hear you say it," he replied with sudden gravity, which it seemed to her he sought to conceal by bending to stir up the fire. "Although your opinion, however kindly rendered, is most definitely in the minority."

The embers flared up into flames, silhouetting his hawkish profile sharply in their light. Lady Leonora judged that no response was required on her part, but her curiosity was piqued. An attractive aura of mystery had begun to settle about the dark gentleman's shoulders like a cloak.

As if he had read her thoughts, he shrugged those broad shoulders inside his finely cut jacket of bath superfine and threw her a devilish grin. "I judge that you, too, find that sleep all too frequently eludes you, ma'am! Perhaps by the very propriety of our conversation, we might lull each other into deep lassitude! May I sit?"

Leonora gestured him toward the chair lately vacated by René, and he seated himself in such a way that his profile was cast into shadow by the flames.

"First," she said, "you must tell me how you identified my insomnia."

"By all the signs a fellow sufferer could identify, ma'am! You have made a long journey today, and, if you will pardon me for saying so, encountered your share of adventures. You should be exhausted, and yet you sit awake until well past midnight, reading a novel that I am fairly certain you mistakenly believed would bore you to sleep."

Lady Leonora smiled ruefully, shaking her head. "Quite correct, alas!" she exclaimed.

The dark gentleman nodded gravely. "Only a fellow sufferer could recognize the symptoms and shudder with empathy." To illustrate his point, he gave a dramatic shudder, and in spite of herself, Lady Leonora burst into laughter.

A few seconds of perfect civility existed between them at that moment, and might have continued had not her companion ventured to ask: had she managed to dispose of her young friend in a suitable fashion?

At once the laughter disappeared from Leonora's eyes and her expression became haughty and severe. "You, sir, are no gentleman, else you would have sought to extricate that poor child from her difficulties at once! Such conduct—or lack of it—is quite inexcusable, you know!"

The dark gentleman raised an eyebrow, looping one well-formed leg over the other. A faint smile played across his features and he shook his head, holding up one finger. "Before you deliver yourself of the set-down you think I deserve, only consider this: the assistance of a single gentleman, rather deep, I admit, in his cups, could have hardly added to the poor girl's credit with mine host. Indeed, what could *I* have done to help her? I would have smirched her reputation far worse than she may have done herself. Indeed, just as you entered, I was considering the pros and cons of intervention—after all, it would hardly do for a schoolgirl to spend a night in the Calais lock! But fortunately for all concerned, *you* appeared and made all right again in a most admirable fashion that somehow left me with the feeling that you are not quite unused to riding roughshod over landlords, Bath misses, and hapless diplomats who run counter to your purposes." His grin was enough to take the sting from his words.

Leonora considered what he had said for a moment, then inclined her head slightly. "I think I shall decide to take that as a compliment," she said at last. "Several years of widowhood have taught me a great deal of pragmatism, if nothing else."

"My condolences, ma'am." The dark gentleman bowed politely.

"My widowhood is of some standing, sir. It

has been many years since I put aside my weeds and went into society again."

"Ah! And so, like all of the polite world, you rush toward Paris and the continent now that Bonaparte is safely away."

"Precisely. I have found London to be a very dull place of late. So, like many another bored and fashionable female, I have decided to seek amusements abroad." There was the slightest hint of dry self-mockery in Leonora's voice. "Unfortunately, I find that travel does not cure my insomnia."

"And indeed, our young friend, I have a feeling, may add to it, if she continues her adventures."

Leonora shrugged. "I hope to have the poor chit safely installed with her godparents in Paris before that happens. It turns out, you see, that Miss Hobart and I have something in common— durance vile in a most dreadful school in Bath! I can only admire her for doing what I lacked the courage to do many years ago and escape!"

"How many times I yearned to break free at Harrow!" the dark gentleman said, leaning comfortably back in his chair and thrusting his hands into his pockets. "Yes, I think one can sympathize with your . . . Miss Hobart, was it? . . . for her escapade. She is only fortunate that she found her good samaritan in you, and not someone else, who might do her harm."

"Such as you?" Leonora ventured.

He made an airy gesture with one hand. "Cut rope, ma'am, cut rope! My reputation may be pitch black, but I hope it may never be said of me that I took advantage of young females of any station and condition! Most unsporting, you know!"

They might, Leonora thought, have been trading light flirtation in any London drawing room. "You know, I wonder why it should be that I have never before encountered you," she said aloud.

The dark gentleman shrugged lightly. "The loss, I assure you, is mine. I would imagine that you travel in circles of fashion and society, while I, ma'am, have confined myself more to those worlds of politics and diplomacy. If you were to frequent Lady Castlereagh's rather than Lady Jersey's—well, then our paths might have crossed before!"

"Perhaps. But you are quite right, that I have no interest at all in politics or diplomacy. I blush to admit that I am hideously fashionable, and care only for the latest styles."

He gave her a penetrating look. "Somehow, I think that I must doubt that, ma'am. I think that you must be interested in a great deal more than the turn of a ruffle or the latest crim. con., and that it suits your purposes to allow the world to believe otherwise."

Leonora smiled lazily. If she had possessed a fan at that moment, she would have used it to advantage. "Perhaps," she admitted with downcast eyes.

"Ah," said the dark gentleman, and there was a space of comfortable silence between them.

"And," Leonora said at last, propping her chin in her hands, "I suppose that you are traveling in connection with politics and diplomacy?"

"You are a most perceptive sort of female, ma'am!" he replied with a grin. "I am attached to Lord Castlereagh's staff, and am on my way to Vienna for the Congress. Or at least I was until I was waylaid by my first taste of good French brandy in many years." He shook his head, pressing two fingers against his forehead. "I must confess that brandy is one of my many weaknesses, else I should not have presented such an unfortunate picture this afternoon—or indeed at this very moment!"

Leonora was forced to laugh at the droll expression he made.

"The Congress, ma'am, promises to be the highlight of the winter season! All Europe will be there, decked out in jewels and medals and ready to celebrate the peace. Shall I expect to see you there?"

Leonora shook her head. "No, I think not. I have no connections in that world. The only purpose of my journey is to avoid boredom. Like an old dog, it nips at my heels always," she added a trifle cynically.

Their eyes met for a moment, and Leonora saw something in the depths of his that forced her to drop her gaze.

If Lady Leonora Ware were capable of blushing, she might have done so. Instead she said, in a voice that held a vague, trembling edge, "We have not been properly introduced, you know. I am Lady Leonora Ware. And you are . . . ?"

"Umberto. Well, that is to say, *everyone* calls me Umberto, from Prinny down to my valet. But he don't call me Umberto. He calls me Mr. Umberto—"

The effect of his words could not have been more electric. "D-did you say *Umberto*? You are, then, Umberto Roberston-Durand, Marques of Durand?"

He bowed. "I have that honor, my lady," he said.

"Ware, sir, Lady Leonora Ware. Perhaps you did not catch my name the first time. Surely you cannot have forgotten so soon?"

His strong jaw hardened. "Good God!" he muttered darkly. "You are Dick's widow?"

Leonora drew herself up to her full height. "You could have no way of knowing, of course, but yes, I am Crafty Dick's widow." She grasped his lapels. "The widow of the man you killed, my lord Umberto!"

2

FOR A MOMENT, neither of them moved.

Then Umberto turned toward the mirror. "I think, my lady, that you have disarranged my cravat," he said in a carefully controlled voice.

Slowly Leonora sank into a chair, attempting without a great deal of success to collect her wits. "Forgive me! But the shock of meeting you . . . and in such circumstances . . ."

"In my own defense, Lady Leonora, I may only say that all that passed between Dick and me was strictly according to the *Code Duello* and witnessed by several gentlemen of impeccable honor."

"Dueling," Leonora sighed. "Is there anything more odious! To awake and find oneself a widow because of a duel—a most terrible experience, sir!"

"Honor had to be satisfied, my lady," he said to the mirror, his lips set in a thin line.

"Dick challenged me, and I had no choice but to accept."

"Honor! It was little better than a brothel brawl!" Leonora exclaimed.

"The incident, my lady, occurred at Crockford's. A most respectable gaming establishment. Hardly, as you say, a brothel."

"I think that no one could know better than I that Richard had many faults, but I assure you, sir, that cheating at cards was not among them. He lacked the skill—*that is,* he was far too deep a player to do something so dishonorable!" Lady Leonora bit her lower lip, regretting her hasty tongue.

But if Umberto had caught it, he gave no indication, only lifted his shoulders slightly, then dropped them again. "I am sorry to have stumbled upon something that must cause you a great deal of pain, Lady Leonora," he said stiffly. "But please recall that Dick had been my friend since we were at Harrow. Do you think my sleepless nights are the result of my many self-indulgences?"

"I would not pretend to know," Lady Leonora replied, dropping her gaze to examine her fingers. "I only know that I awoke one morning to find myself a widow."

"If I could recall that one single night in my life, I would give anything," Umberto mused. "Particularly now that I know what pain it has given to someone whose high esteem I wish I could have won."

He turned around to look at her, and it seemed to Leonora that his gaze stabbed her through the heart. She looked away, unable to speak.

"I will only say, Lady Leonora, that there were circumstances which demanded action. I tried to be as discreet as possible, but your husband would have none of it. He had dipped deeply that night, both in wagers and wine. He chose to see an offense where I had only meant to assist him as quietly as possible away from a public scandal. He said that I had accused him of cheating, and that his honor could only be satisfied by a duel. He chose pistols, even though he knew that I was a far better shot than he—it was almost suicide! I knew he had been drinking heavily, and I thought to delope, as I thought that Dick would, when he recovered his senses and realized what foolishness it all was. . . ."

"But he did not. And you did not delope. And I was married six months before I was a widow," Leonora finished.

A corner of Umberto's mouth twisted upward. "On the field that morning, I meant to delope, but there were circumstances . . . Had I known you then, Lady Leonora, I assure you, I would have willingly taken a bullet in my breast rather than . . ." Umberto shook his head, pushing a hand through his dark hair.

Leonora rose and paced the room. She hesitated before the window, looking out into the black and rainy night. "My parents chose Richard for me. I was not very long out of school and in the beginning of my first season. My father was also a heavy gamester, you see. I think that he had met Richard in Crockford's or

Watier's. But Richard's pockets were full of brass, and Papa's were not. It was my duty. I married Richard to save the family." She turned and regarded Umberto with her gray eyes.

"I think I understand," he murmured.

"You see," Leonora rushed on, "Richard loved toys. Phaetons, guns, horses, all the toys that men love to possess. For him, I was just another toy, I think." A thin line creased her forehead. "And when he was through with his toys, he threw them aside for new ones. I think when he died, he was just about to throw me aside for something—or someone—new." She drew herself up to her full height. "I only tell you these things, Lord Umberto, so that you may not lose sleep at night on my account." Her smile was sophisticated and brittle.

Lord Umberto bowed. "I understand, my lady," he said, "and I thank you."

Leonora inclined her head slightly and drew her train across the floor. "And now, I think that I had best retire to bed. I have a long journey ahead of me, and I doubt that sleep will elude me any further this night."

"Lady Leonora!"

She paused at the doorway, looking back at him quizzically. Lord Umberto's face was half in shadow, giving his features a slightly devilish cast. "I only wish that we might have met sooner— or at least under more pleasant circumstances."

"I, too, wish the same thing," Leonora acknowledged, lingering for a second to study him. "Perhaps we might have become friends."

"How could it be that you, of all people,

should be that one person . . ." Umberto said urgently, bitterly.

"The one person above all others . . ." Leonora sighed, shaking her head. "This must be moonlight, or wine, or some vice of Calais's doing! Such things do not happen to me, for I am said, you know, to have no heart, much less a heart that I could cast upon the man who—"

"A sweet madness! All my life I have looked for you in the faces of a thousand different women, in a hundred countries . . ."

No more words passed between them. Like magnet and steel, they were drawn into each other's arms, and Leonora, always so strong, felt herself surrender to his embrace with a sigh of release.

They stood together in the darkness for a very long time, clinging to each other as if they had finally come home, content to be together.

On the landing, the old clock chimed slowly twelve times, its wooden works clicking and groaning with each movement.

"Vienna will be a fairy tale. All Europe will be there to dance and glitter," Umberto whispered.

Reluctantly Leonora disentangled herself. "Would that I could be there to dance with you! But it is not to be, you know. Not for you and me, my dear Umberto. Sooner or later, the music will stop, and the dancers will go home, and men will tire of their toys. And we will both wonder at what a very narrow escape we had from folly!"

Standing on tiptoe, she kissed his cheek,

and drawing up her train, mounted the stairs without looking back.

She did not dare.

If Leonora had expected to see Lord Umberto, sober and perhaps chastised in the bright light of day, she was disappointed, for he was up and gone long before her party had made its appearance at the breakfast table.

If Lady Leonora seemed unnaturally somber and pensive as she sipped at her tea, Jane Hobart was too full of lively chatter that she more than made up for the silence of her benefactress. In high anticipation of travel, in such glamorous company, she prattled on at René while polishing off a breakfast of omelets, sausages, croissants, strawberry-rhubarb tarts, pâté, and two pots of tea.

Leonora's enormous traveling coach was lumbering away from the inn yard when the landlord, red-faced and out of breath, puffed up to her window, waving frantically.

"Now what?" Lady Leonora said irritably as René let the glass down and poked his finely styled curls into the morning air.

"For Madame," the proprietor puffed, thrusting a bunch of violets through the window in Leonora's direction. "From the English gentleman who departed this morning."

René, considerably amused, translated this message to his employer, and Jane Hobart's eyes grew as round as saucers.

"What a conquest you have made, my lady!" she exclaimed in tones of admiration.

With what dignity she could muster, Lady Leonora accepted the nosegay, wondering to what lengths Umberto must have gone to procure violets out of season in Calais. She would have been less than human, and less than female, if she had not held them beneath her nose to conceal the tiny smile that parted her lips. It was only when she saw her two companions watching her with unconcealed curiosity that she collected herself, very properly thanked the landlord, and instructed René to have the coachman drive on.

René leaned back against the squabs and crossed one elegantly shod leg across the other, doing his very best not to grin knowingly at his employer. Miss Hobart, however, was unrestrained, leaning forward in her seat and disarranging her chipstraw bonnet and its pink ribbands in an effort to peer more closely at the violets.

Leonora, as if to demonstrate her lack of interest in the subject, tossed the nosegay carelessly on the seat beside her, making a great display of carefully working on her tan gloves, one finger at a time as she watched the autumn fields busy with the harvesting of hops, roll by.

"I had quite forgotten how lovely the countryside could be in France," she remarked.

She decided that nothing would be gained by discussing the events of the previous night with either of her companions. It was all in the past, and she would never see Lord Umberto again.

Alas, added a small voice inside herself.

3

WITH HIS USUAL expertise, René had managed to secure Lady Leonora and her party a very fine suite of rooms just off Place Vendôme. When they arrived at Le Narvonne two days later, he was pleased to escort his ladies through the elegant hallways of the hotel to their rooms, assuring his mistress that all would be of the very finest, just as she was used to at home.

"Indeed," Lady Leonora murmured, for the first face her eye fell upon when the door of her suite was opened was that of her dour and unsmiling abigail, Strawbridge, the tip of whose long and pointed nose always turned pink when she was agitated.

The tip of Strawbridge's nose turned bright red when she saw the disheveled young person her mistress brought into the room. That very same nose was already severely out of joint that my lady had chosen to send her ahead to Paris with the baggage coach, for she believed that her mistress was totally lost without her, and viewed the good René with suspicion for his exotic French ways, so different from those of her native Kent.

Nor did Lady Leonora disappoint her by exclaiming, "Strawbridge! Good God, I never thought I would be glad to see you, but I am, after such a journey! Have you arranged everything just as I would wish, then?"

Strawbridge dipped a bony curtsy. "Of course. I have not been in your service for the past six years for nothing, my lady," she replied tartly, casting a severe eye up and down Leonora's rumpled person. "Best let me remove that bonnet, my lady, before you crush any more of those lovely green plumes."

While Leonora stood and allowed Strawbridge to fuss over her, René turned to Jane and winked. "One would never know that they are *devoted* to each other, *hein?*" he whispered, and Jane, looking about the gilt-and-ebony Napoleonic decor of the reception room, barely heard him. It was all quite in the first style of *élégance moderne*, and quite, quite different from the grim gray environment of Miss Gunnerston's Seminary for Young Females in Bath.

As Strawbridge undid the strings that held Leonora's bonnet firmly beneath her chin, she shook her head and whispered, "My lady! This hotel is full of *foreigners!*"

Leonora suppressed a smile, since this was, after all, the dour Kentish woman's first trip abroad. "Well, we are in France, you know, and France is full of French people."

"Who speak no English, mind!" Strawbridge breathed, unbuttoning Leonora's pelisse with a button hook. She shook her head. "It's enough to give one a turn, my lady! But the fashions— cut down to here, and up to there, all bosoms and ankles showing!" She shook her head again.

"Pray do not fuss so with me, Strawbridge! I know too well what I must look like without you to see to me! If you please, you will look to Miss Hobart, who . . . who has had a rather unfortunate accident on the road and depends upon us to restore her to her godparents, Lord and Lady Somerville, here in Paris."

Strawbridge reluctantly cast an eye over Miss Hobart, taking in her slightly crushed chipstraw hat, her sadly creased drab pelisse, and her muddy jean boots. The tip of her nose turned scarlet.

"I depend upon you to make Miss Hobart presentable before we restore her to her godparents, Strawbridge," Lady Leonora said.

Strawbridge sniffed, and Miss Hobart, for once silenced, meekly followed the abigail, with her portmanteau, into the bedroom.

"Well, René!" Leonora sighed, crossing to the window case to look down into Place Vendôme. "We have reached Paris safe and sound, have we not?"

"Indeed, my lady," he replied, crossing the room to stand beside her, looking down into the street. "It is a most amusing thought, madame, that I am having. Only consider that when last

I was in this city, I was a little aristo, smuggled away beneath a cartload of cabbages. Twenty years later, I return as a servant. It is a most shatter-brained world, is it not?"

"It is indeed, René," Leonora agreed. "But you know, with Bonaparte gone, and the Bourbons returning to the throne, it may be that you will regain your titles and your land."

"Perhaps. It will be strange, to have servants and not to be one, madame. We shall see what happens. It may be that we shall grow gray together."

"It may be. But I would prefer to see that you are restored to what you have lost, you know."

René shrugged, and Leonora decided not to press the issue.

While René might be zealous in managing her personal life, he was quite secretive about his own, and Leonora had long ago learned not to inquire.

"Paris," René said thoughtfully. "I think, madame, that it might be wise if I were to seek Lord and Lady Somerville before dinnertime, or our young friend will exhaust our letter of credit on her board."

Leonora laughed. "Yes, perhaps that would be a good thing. If Miss Hobart's father has learned of her disappearance, he will doubtless be mad with worry, and the sooner we can place her into the hands of a responsible couple, the better it will be. I am not used to this role of duenna, bear-leading chits about the continent!"

She sat down at the little writing desk in the

corner and quickly penned a note in her long, uneven scrawl. "There! That should hold us for the time being. But in case it does not, see what plays there might be at the theaters, and if you can find a Molière or something else suitable for a young girl, hire a box."

René bowed. "Very good, my lady. I shall see what can be done."

After making certain that Miss Hobart was ensconced in a tub of hot water and that Strawbridge, with cluckings of the tongue, was pressing out a demure straw silk dinner dress retrieved from the jumble that was Jane's portmanteau, Leonora retired to her own room, where she retrieved a crumpled nosegay of violets from her reticule and pressed them beneath her nose. Using a little water from the handbasin, she filled a vase and placed them on a small table. Then, after staring at the wilted nosegay for some minutes, she heaved a sigh, propped her chin on her hand, and gazed out the window at Paris, musing to herself that so far, her trip had been nothing as she had pictured it.

"But at least it has not been dull," she reminded herself aloud, and rose, with a little shake of her skirts, to ring the bell for the porter, in order to choose a dinner menu.

Some hours later, she had bathed, and was allowing Strawbridge to dress her hair, when the maid gave another sniff.

"What is it now, Strawbridge?" she sighed, examining her face in the mirror for wrinkles that had not yet appeared.

"It's just that I can't understand, when you was so specific about filling up the *soote* with flowers, as to why you would thrust that wilted, nasty old bunch of violets into a vase and set them on your nightstand."

"If I wanted you to know, I would have told you, wouldn't I, Strawbridge?" Lady Leonora responded, and received a sharp tug on her hair for her pains.

"Drat those rats," Strawbridge said quickly, a triumphant gleam in her eye. "You see what happens, Lady Leonora, when I let you out of my sight for more than a day!"

"*I* know why," Jane said in a singsong voice, turning from the mirror where she was pirouetting with one of Leonora's cashmere shawls over her simple silk dress.

"You think you do, miss!" said Strawbridge in such boding tones that Jane instantly fell silent.

"I think that I just heard the door," Leonora said quickly. "It must be René. Jane, will you go and let him in?"

"Of course," Jane said, thrusting her tongue out at Strawbridge's back as she left the room.

"I cannot help but mistrust that young person, my lady," Strawbridge muttered, thrusting a silver bodkin into Leonora's auburn curls. "If you ask me, she's no runaway but an *adventuress*!"

"Oh, really!" Lady Leonora said, as the abigail held the mirror so that she could see the back of her head. Leonora nodded her approval of her hair, done *à la Meduse*, if not of Miss Strawbridge's declaration.

"Strawbridge, you are so respectable that

you would not know an adventuress if she came up and bit you on the nose!" Leonora said firmly, rising from the chair and removing her dressing gown.

"Even so, my lady, that young person is too cheeky by half for my tastes! You were not very much older than she when you first came to me, my lady, and you were well-mannered in every way." From the bed, she picked up a dinner dress of *margaruite* satin, décolleté, and trimmed at slashed sleeve and banded hem with ruching and Brussels lace, and slipped it over Lady Leonora's head, shaking out the skirt as the gown tumbled into place on her mistress. "This is not a dress that packs well, so much pressing, even though I wrapped it in silver paper and tissue very special."

"Young *lady*, Strawbridge, if you please. Not young *person*. She must be respectable, for she went to Miss Gunnerston's, which is a most respectable place, if nothing else can be said for it." Leonora pulled down the neckline of her gown and held her breath as Strawbridge did up the buttons.

Strawbridge sniffed. "Just as you like, my lady. After all, I've only been with you these past six years, and before that, I was with the Duchess of Carmody, rest her soul . . ." Coming about to the front, she hitched up Leonora's neckline. ". . . So what would *I* know compared to someone you only met in most peculiar circumstances a few days ago?"

"What indeed?" Leonora asked, as Strawbridge opened her jewel case and held a pearl-

and-diamond necklace against her mistress's skin.
Leonora nodded, slipping on the matching
bracelet. "Why, Strawbridge, I do believe you're
jealous!"

"Jealous? Me, my lady? Whatever of?"
Strawbridge fastened a pair of pearl-and-diamond droplets into Leonora's ears.

"Why, of Miss Hobart, of course," Lady
Leonora replied, holding out an arm so that
Strawbridge could work a long kid glove up its
length while she gave a loud and meaningful
sniff, and the tip of her nose burned crimson.

"Reeely, my lady," she said, stepping back
to observe her handiwork.

"Really, Strawbridge," Lady Leonora replied, examining herself from all views in the
triptych mirror. "Which is quite ridiculous, since
we will have her off our hands by tomorrow at
the latest, when her godparents come and fetch
her away." Leonora pulled her bodice down an
inch.

"I wonder," Miss Strawbridge breathed, as
she draped a gauzed, spangled shawl over her
mistress's arms, handed her a beaded reticule in
the shape of an urn, and pulled her bodice up
over her bosom.

"Please do not bother, Strawbridge!" Lady
Leonora snapped, and Strawbridge, realizing
that she had gone too far, merely sniffed again,
remarking that she had never thought that particular shade of *margaruite* was at all becoming
to my lady's fair skin.

"Piffle," Leonora remarked, accepting the
painted chicken-skin fan from Strawbridge's

hands. "Come, Strawbridge! You are always trying to wrap me in cotton wool! I haven't been a green 'un for a good number of years now, you know! A widow becomes quite used to defending herself from toad-eaters and gazetted fortune hunters and all manner of odious mushrooms! Do you not think that I have a sharper eye than all of that?"

"I have always thought my lady to be up to every rig and row in town," Strawbridge admitted reluctantly, for she had a good Kentish woman's dislike of London cant, no matter how fashionable.

"There, now! You may have the rest of the evening off, if you like. You've worked very hard, and I mean to reward you for it all. Strawbridge, you know as well as I do that when I am without you for more than a day, I look a perfect fright."

Somewhat mollified, Strawbridge bowed. But as Leonora swept out of the room, she shook her head, muttering that nothing good would ever come of picking up stray hussies in foreign inns.

What my lady needed, she told the cast-off dressing gown as she picked it up and smoothed out its folds, was a good husband.

In her opinion, my lady had already had a bad one.

Entering the reception room, Leonora saw that a waiter was laying out an excellent repast on the linen cover. With masterful finesse, he removed the covers from succulent dishes, while Jane, looking very much the Bath miss in her simple little straw-colored silk, with only a strand of pearls about her neck, looked on, utterly famished, since she had not eaten anything since tea two hours ago.

Looking at her young companion's slender figure, Leonora wondered if the chit had a hollow leg. She nodded her approval of the bottle of wine the waiter presented for her inspection, and watched as he expertly drew its cork, splashing a little of the Médoc into a glass for her.

"I think we must go on without René," she told Jane, savoring the bittersweet taste of the wine on her tongue. *"Ça fait bien,"* she informed the waiter, who poured out a glass for Jane and filled Lady Leonora's before withdrawing, with several bows, toward the door.

Leonora rather doubtfully watched Jane taste her wine. In her day, schoolgirls had not been allowed more than a taste, and that liberally cut with water, but she supposed things had changed since then. Really, she thought, there was so much that she did not know about the management of Bath misses that she was grateful she would soon be delivering Jane to her godparents, who, presumably, would be equipped to deal with the situation.

But the quality of the dinner was such that even Lady Leonora, who normally took very little interest in her plate, found her appetite piqued, and very soon they were dining off asparagus in truffle sauce, *veau à la Josephine,* tongue in curry sauce, *jambon au fromage,* and sole with onions, together with several removes and the prospect of fruits, cheeses, and *gâteaux* for dessert.

Throughout the meal, Jane chattered on happily, obviously delirious with wine and the idea of doing something as sophisticated as dining with a lady in the first stare of fashion in an elegant Paris hotel.

Leonora sipped at her own wine, amused.

They had just begun to dig their forks into the *gâteaux au chocolat* when René appeared in the doorway, his countenance rather grim as he tossed his high-crowned beaver into a chair and began to strip off his gloves.

"*Alors!*" he said, examining himself in the mirror, patting his perfectly coiffed curls into place. "*Le tout Paris* is a madhouse, my lady!"

"Well, when will Lord and Lady Somerville come and fetch Miss Hobart?" Leonora asked.

"Ah, madame, perhaps never!" René exclaimed dramatically, and both Lady Leonora and Miss Hobart paused over their cake, looking up at him with startled eyes.

René seated himself in a chair with an exhausted sigh, accepting the glass of wine Lady Leonora proffered him and drinking it gratefully. "I went to the residence of Lord and Lady Somerville, on Rue Sauvage, *mais* the shutters were closed and the knocker had been taken down from the door, a very bad sign indeed. I pounded and pounded, however, and eventually roused an ancient and most unpleasant old caretaker who, after I had bribed him a few francs, informed me that the Somervilles had departed an unknown time ago, for an unknown destination, and were expected to return at some unknown time in the future."

"Oh, no!" Jane cried, genuinely dismayed.

"Now, now, let René continue," Lady Leonora advised kindly, laying a hand on Jane's arm.

René nodded, having another jolt of wine. "So then," he continued when he judged his pause to be dramatic enough, "I went to the embassy, since Miss Hobart had mentioned that Lord Somerville had some connection there. The embassy, it would seem, cares very little for any stray godchildren who might appear in Paris, and could only promise that they might have a direction for the Somervilles within a fortnight, but it was suspected that they had gone either to Lake Como to take the air or to Vienna *pour le congrès.*"

From an inner pocket he withdrew a sheaf of cream-colored notes. "Your messages, madame," he announced, handing them to Lady Leonora. "It would seem that *le tout Londres* has descended upon Paris."

Lady Leonora glanced through the seals with an increasing frown before tossing them carelessly aside. "Good God!" she said, more to herself than to her companions. "It would seem that I am pursued to Paris by the wit and *ton* of society—precisely the sort of people that I fled London to escape!"

Miss Hobart opened her eyes very wide to think that anyone would escape from fashionable society, but René merely shook his head and dipped into another pocket. "And," he announced, "a box for tonight's performance of Molière, which I know you will forgive me if I do not attend. I have had a most exhausting day. Indeed, I believe that my first day of return to Paris must be as exhausting as the day I left beneath that cartload of cabbages. I should very much like to meet this Lord and Lady Somerville, Miss Hobart, so that I may inform them of my opinions of their ill-managed household. Imagine anyone taking down their knocker without leaving instructions with the caretaker as to how they may be reached."

"I imagine things are different in Paris," Jane said soothingly, but by the way in which she was twisting her napkin, her own agitation over this unforeseen state of affairs was made plain.

René smiled. "Do not worry, *ma petite ma'mselle!* Lady Leonora is the most complete hand!" he told her reassuringly.

Lady Leonora privately wondered if she was, indeed, the most complete hand, but merely smiled vaguely at both of them as she scooped through her stack of invitations.

"Come now," my lady said bracingly, "it is not the end of the world, you know. We shall think of something. Now, eat your dinner."

Jane's face cleared. "Oh, you *are* the most complete hand, Lady Leonora!" she said adoringly, setting to her dinner with gusto.

Lady Leonora wondered again if she were, indeed, the most complete hand, for she was at a standstill as to what to do with a young girl in Paris. Certainly none of the entertainments she had planned for herself were suitable for a chit not yet out of the schoolroom, and those of her friends who were currently in the City of Light were not, she was certain, of the sort that one would introduce to a Bath miss, as much for their sakes as hers.

"Well, something will arrive," she murmured beneath her breath, pouring herself another glass of wine.

And sure enough, something did.

4

THE COMÉDIE FRANÇAISE, like most theaters in post-Bonaparte France, was poorly lit by limestone footlights, and the atmosphere was almost foggy from the cheap oil used in the lamps. The cavernous old building reeked equally of smoke and onions, and the gilt N's and Bonapartist bee, hastily eradicated from the boxes and the proscenium, were yet visible beneath a coat of whitewash. And yet, to Leonora's discerning eye, the French themselves were as elegant and fashionable as ever, turned out in the latest French styles and in great numbers to see *Les Femmes Savantes* with Mlle. George, only recently better known as Bonaparte's favorite mistress, in the lead role. Clearly the French felt the need to escape from dreary reality as much as the rest of a war-weary Europe, for the theater was packed as full as it could be.

My lady could only be aware that she and

Miss Hobart made a very charming picture in their box, and she settled herself in her seat, disposed of her shawl and reticule with practiced grace, raised her opera glasses, and proceeded to gaze about with casual interest, studying the latest in French fashion. In her survey, she noted that the audience was not exclusively French, for she saw a great many English and Russian faces among those present.

For her part, Jane, whose previous theatrical experience was limited to visits to Astley's Amphitheater, felt very sophisticated indeed, looking around with a great deal of interest and very little comprehension of the admiring looks she was receiving from the gentlemen of several nations. Perhaps it could be said that this was fortunate for Miss Hobart's innocence, as the tone of some of their minds was not at all lofty.

Suddenly there was a minor stir, and the orchestra played the sonorous anthem of the *ancien régime*. Everyone rose to their feet, and all eyes were focused upon the large box draped with white silk and adorned with the Bourbon lily as quite the largest person Leonora had ever seen made his ponderous way to his chair, where he stood waving and bowing with the utmost affability toward the audience.

"Why, that is Louis XVIII!" Jane whispered to Leonora. "How much fatter he has grown since I was taken to see him when I was a very little girl at Hartwell! And the lady is the Duchesse D'Angoulême—so very haughty!—and the other fat gentleman is the Comte D'Artois!"

"That is the man the czar put on the throne

of France?" Leonora whispered incredulously. "He ought to be in Astley's, not on a throne!"

Jane hid a giggle behind her fan. And indeed, the restored monarch did have something of the buffoon about him, so vacuous was his smile and so clumsy was his girth as his chair was thrust beneath his ample bottom by a pair of anxious servants.

The sigh of relief was almost audible as he sank into the cushions and smiled affably at his companions.

Only when that crisis had passed did the curtain rise. Mlle. George, approaching forty-five, Leonora guessed, but still a great beauty, made her entrance to enthusiastic applause from the French and the putting up of a great many sets of opera glasses by the English, curious to see, at last, the female who had enjoyed the favors of the Little Corsican for so many years.

The understanding of the French language existing between Lady Leonora and Miss Hobart, educated as they had been by that most inadequate preceptress, Miss Gunnerston, could have filled a teacup. So they could only follow the plot very sketchily, losing their interest from time to time in some detail of a costume or some more interesting drama between a fashionable buck and an orange girl in the pit.

Indeed, very few members of the audience were giving the comedy on the stage much attention. One did not, after all, come to the theater to see the play. One came to see and be seen, to gossip and become a cause for gossip, to make an assignation or break one, to flirt with the orange girls or the handsome gentleman across the way, or, like Lady Leonora, to study the latest fashions of the season.

Indeed, Leonora was making mental notes upon the elaborate toilette of the lady across the way when she half-heard Jane's muffled exclamation of surprise and felt rather than saw someone slide into the seat beside her.

Expressively snapping her fan, Lady Leonora turned, ready to administer a blistering setdown to the intruder.

But the words died away on her lips as she found herself pinned by the dark gaze of Lord Umberto, handsome and impeccable in corbeau-colored evening dress. A devilish grin spread across his saturnine features as he took Leonora's hand into his own and lifted it to his lips.

"Forgive my intrusion, my lady," he said smoothly, only the faintest hint of mischief in his voice. "But when I saw you and the Bath mi—that is to say, Miss Hobart!—seated here, I knew that I must come and pay my respects instantly!"

Two bright spots of color flooded into Lady Leonora's cheeks. "I thought, sir, that we had *agreed* . . ." she whispered fiercely, struggling without success to release her hand from his powerful fingers.

"Ah. Unfortunately, Lady Leonora, promises were made to be broken, were they not?" His smile was devastating, and in spite of herself, Leonora felt the corners of her mouth lifting upward. "You see before you, madam, only a diplomatic emissary obeying the orders of his chief of mission. In short, his Grace of Wellington has requested me to beg your acquaintance for him."

"Wellington!" Jane breathed, her eyes very wide. "The Hero of the Peninsula!"

Umberto's smile increased. "Precisely. Save that he is now the ambassador to France and my superior. Please, Lady Leonora, I beg of you, have mercy upon Old Hook. Caroline Lamb has taken it into her head to pursue him through Paris, and the poor man is driven to distraction. It is hoped that should he express *interest* in another female, it might discourage Lady Caroline's . . . ah, unwelcome interest."

Leonora inclined her head slightly to one side, a thin smile of comprehension dawning across her features. "Caro Lamb. Oh, Lord!" she sighed. "Does that woman never tire of making a cake of herself?"

"It would seem not," Umberto agreed, shaking his head. "Although what she expects to accomplish with Old Hook is beyond my ken. She haunts the residence and the embassy, waylaying him upon every opportunity, until it has become a sore embarrassment to everyone. Cannot her family do anything with her, I wonder."

"It would appear not. Poor Charles Lamb, to be buckled to such a one as she!" Leonora sighed again. "I should be honored if the duke would wish to come to our box."

"Just as you say, madam," Umberto agreed,

bowing low over her hand and holding it just a second longer than necessary.

As promised, the duke made his appearance at the entr'acte, and was as affable and civil as Lady Leonora could have wished, standing upon no ceremony and deeply grateful to Lady Leonora for agreeing to make his acquaintance. It was clear that he had an eye for an attractive female of whatever age, for he divided his attention equally between Lady Leonora and Miss Hobart. Indeed, he chatted so easily with that young miss that she was very soon quite at ease with him. Upon discovering she was the daughter of his old friend Sir Julian, he was at once curious to know how she came to be in Paris with Lady Leonora Ware. The entire story came spilling out, and if the duke was amused, only the merest twitch of his lips betrayed his emotions as he listened carefully to Jane's story and her present predicament.

While the duke was amusing himself with Miss Hobart, Lord Umberto seized the chance to speak with Lady Leonora.

"How do you enjoy Paris, then?" he asked lazily, leaning back against the box and watching her from beneath his eyelids.

"One finds oneself in the most wretched tangles that one did not at all expect!" Leonora confessed ruefully. "Now, if you please, my lord Umberto, tell me what I am to do with a Bath miss in Paris!"

"Oh, I think you shall contrive, ma'am!" Umberto replied lazily. "After all, you rescued the chit from Les Trois Poissons, did you not?"

"But I thought that I should have to bring her to Paris only! How was I to count upon these Somerville people going off to Vienna, of all places?"

Her hand was suddenly seized in his own, and she looked up to see him looking back down at her, a lazy smile flickering across his face. "This means that I shall be able to see all the more of you, dear ma'am. I can think of nothing I should enjoy more than a chance to further our acquaintance."

Leonora flushed, attempting to withdraw her hand from his. But he held her fast by him, his face dark and serious, all laughter gone from his rugged features. Their eyes met.

"You forget, sir," Leonora managed to say after a moment, her voice slightly breathless, "that there are circumstances which would prevent any person of *sensibility* from attempting to pursue my acquaintance under such circumstances! People are watching!"

"If they are watching, it is only because you and Miss Hobart make such a charming picture. But only consider, my dear Lady Leonora, that I am without sensibility when I have set my mind upon something. And I am generally held to get what I want!" The twinkle was back in his eye.

"Then only consider my reputation!" Leonora hissed. "Do you think it does me well to be seen in an opera box with the man who killed my husband?"

"Perhaps not, but it does do you an enormous amount of credit to be seen with the Duke of Wellington, does it not?" Umberto replied smoothly, one dark eyebrow raised sardonically.

Leonora fought down the impulse to slap his face. Instead, she tried to withdraw his hand from her own, only to find herself held fast.

"Release me, if you please, sir!" she hissed. "This is hardly appropriate!"

"Ah, but it gives me so much pleasure," Umberto replied smoothly.

"And does you very little credit!" Leonora snapped. "You are the most vile, wretched, odious creature—"

"Aren't I just?" Umberto replied with total sincerity. "It really is too bad for me, you know."

Propriety demanded Lady Leonora suppress the quite inappropriate urge to laugh. "Arrogant, selfish, odious man!" she exclaimed, snapping her fan.

"Ah, yes, how lovely to be me," Umberto remarked airily. "Yes, I am all of those things and more, I assure you, ma'am. But only consider how very interesting my many, many bad qualities make me! I am given to understand that there is no one who appeals to females quite so much as such a sad scapegrace as I. Do you not even feel up to the challenge?"

Leonora cast him a sideways glance that spoke volumes for her feelings, and fanned her flushed cheeks furiously, doing her best to control the way in which the corners of her lips sought to curve upward.

"Ah, but swiftly, dear madam! I see Talleyrand himself, and by the look of him, he means to amble in the direction of this box!"

In spite of herself, Leonora did look, and Umberto seized the opportunity to slide his arm about her slender waist.

"Now, Lady Leonora, you must admit that *that* is much better. You see, we have diverted M. All-Things-to-All-Men to the box of the Marquise d'Osmond. Let *her* deal with him, if she will!"

"Perhaps I should be delighted to meet the prince," Leonora said, firmly disengaging Umberto's arm from about her waist and placing his hand back in his own lap.

In a very few minutes, her wish was granted, for Talleyrand, Prince de Benevent, accompanied by several of his aides, had made his way into the box and was conversing with Wellington and Umberto in rapid-fire French, all the while scanning, it seemed to Lady Leonora, herself and Miss Hobart with an air of great appreciation of the sort that only the French seemed to possess. Even though he was charming, Leonora thought that she could sense a mind that was always working, always scheming, always plotting behind his smooth facade.

Although she was not at all political, she sensed, too, that she was being appraised in terms of her position within this gathering, and could almost wonder what ploys rose and fell as the duke and the prince made apparently idle conversation.

Yes, he was very charming, as everyone said he was, but still there was something about him that she could not quite like. She was relieved when he bowed over her hand and that of Jane, bowed to the duke and Umberto, and took his leave, trailed by his aides.

"What an excessively odd little man," Jane said naively. "One was brought up to think him a monster second only to Bonaparte himself, and yet, your grace, he is only a little man with a club foot and a powdered wig!"

Wellington's lips turned upward in a grim smile. "Not a man to be underestimated, my dear Miss Hobart! Not at all! I would never dream of turning my back upon him for one moment!"

"Nor, it appears, would the czar," murmured Umberto.

Wellington unbent his long form from the chair. "The second act begins. A most charming interlude, ladies, and I thank you for your company. I am to give a ball at the residence on Thursday, and I would be honored if you would grace it with your presence."

"An excellent idea!" Umberto seconded his chief of mission.

But Leonora was thinking on her feet. "A most delightful invitation, your grace, and I wish that we could take you up on your very kind offer. But you see, Miss Hobart is not yet out and . . . and I must of course take her on to Vienna to restore her to her father!"

A bit of gentle pressure against the instep of Jane's satin slipper precluded any protest from that damsel.

"A great pity that we shall lose you in Paris, Lady Leonora!" the duke said. "This city is almost entirely devoid of lovely females. They tend to run more along the lines of Emily Castlereagh! However, in a few short weeks we shall meet again, for the Congress opens, and there, I expect, we may see a time!"

"Unfortunately, I shall stay in Vienna only long enough to place Miss Hobart in her father's charge," Leonora said quickly. "But I know that it will be a great pity to miss the Congress."

"Where do you go, Lady Leonora?" Lord Umberto asked lazily.

Leonora looked at him from beneath her lashes. "Oh, I suppose I shall go wherever René's good genius decides. I understand that Copenhagen is quite lovely. Or perhaps Naples." She shrugged.

"A great pity! In a fortnight's time, all the world will be gathered in Vienna!"

Ceremoniously the two gentlemen made their farewells. As Lady Leonora and Jane settled back into their seats and the curtain rose, Jane glanced over at her mentor. "Why did you refuse the duke's invitation? It would mean staying on in Paris only a few more days. I would not mind, although I must say, Lady Leonora, that it is above all things kind of you to take me to Papa in Vienna!"

Leonora toyed with her fan in her lap. "Oh, I thought it best to depress the attentions of my lord Umberto before he became even more encroaching."

Miss Hobart gave her a very odd look, but decided to hold her tongue. With a little sigh, she returned to the play.

Leonora closed her eyes. Yes, she thought to herself, better to leave now, to make a quick escape, than to fall into the unthinkable trap of falling in love with the man who had killed her husband in a duel. . . .

5

THE MORNING LIGHT was still thin and gray when Lady Leonora Ware and her party climbed into her heavy traveling carriage embossed with the Ware coat of arms upon the door, equipped with every comfort, and rolled through the awakening streets of Paris, on their way to Vienna.

The ill-assorted occupants were not unnaturally silent at that hour of the morning, each absorbed with his or her own thoughts as the heavy vehicle jounced over the ancient cobbles.

Miss Hobart, seated beside her patroness, was peering intently through the micah windows, intent upon taking in every sight and sound that the City of Light had to offer that morning, and thinking on to Vienna and a reunion with her father, whom she had not seen in a great many months.

René, who had returned in the early hours

of the morning, having completed some mysterious mission of his own, had greeted Lady Leonora's announcement that they would be departing for Vienna that very morning without turning a hair. When he might well have been sleeping, he had quickly made all the necessary arrangements for the journey, and now dozed contentedly in his corner, oblivious of the rumble and jerk of the heavy vehicle, dreaming perhaps of all the delights to be found in Austria.

Strawbridge, seated primly opposite her mistress, my lady's traveling jewel case of tortoise and morocco leather clutched firmly in her lap, gave from time to time an audible sniff, thus expressing her disapproval of these sudden fits and jaunts my lady had seen fit to undertake since the young person had attached herself to the party.

It was Strawbridge's dark opinion that not only was there no such thing as a Sir Julian Hobart, but that Vienna was full of even more foreigners who were even less civilized than the French. It was understood that there would be Russians there, among other persons, and after the disastrous visit of the czar and the Grand Duchess Catherine to London last spring, she was convinced that all Russians were barbarians. It was not at all what a good Kentish Englishwoman was used to, and she gave another sniff, just to let Lady Leonora catch her drift.

But Lady Leonora's mind was not on Miss Strawbridge's problems. Her plans for a sentimental journey had been quite overset, and it took all of her self-control not to wish dark things upon the dark head of Lord Umberto. Bad enough that the odious man should refuse her all aid and assistance in Calais, but last night's scene at the opera passed all comprehension. He must be mad, to think that she, Leonora Ware, would set up a flirtation with the man who had killed her husband in a duel.

Admittedly, her affection for Richard had turned from tepid to nil in the six months of their marriage. Indeed, it had been her experiences with him that had decided that she should never marry again, if marriage was such a complete hell as he had made it for her. Was it an offense against all sensibility to admit to herself how relieved she had been when she heard the news that he had capped an evening of dissipations by engaging to fight a duel with the best shot in England? Certainly it had put an end to her misery, and freed her from the tyranny of Lord Richard Ware.

Such thoughts were unthinkable, and yet she must think them, for encountering Umberto thus had dredged up things from her past that she thought long buried.

She could not have lingered in Paris, nor accepted the duke's invitation. To have done so would only lead to seeing Umberto again, and she did not want to see Umberto again.

No, no, she thought, her gloved hands curling in her lap. She did want to see him again. And she felt that she could not. She must admit to herself that she found him attractive, *too* attractive. And she had no doubt that he found her so—he had certainly wasted no time in making that clear enough in the opera box.

Ruthlessly she suppressed a little smile that rose to her lips, recollecting the scene. What folly would it be to become involved with a man so dangerous to know? A man who had killed her husband in a duel.

That alone made it all impossible, and yet she could not quite suppress a trace of wistfulness for what might have been.

Why must she find him, of all men, so attractive? After her disastrous marriage with Richard, she had sworn never to involve herself with another man again.

Well, it was all behind her. She was on her way to Vienna and would never see Umberto again.

Tilting her toque a little over one eye, she put a finger against her cheek, gazing out at the passing morning scenes of Paris.

Although England had been engaged in a war to the death with Bonaparte for nearly a generation, the physical effects of that war had never touched the green and peaceful shores of Britain. But the closer they came to the border between France and the Confederation of the Rhine, the bleaker and more desolate became the landscapes they passed.

Whole villages had been laid to waste, the inhabitants hollow-eyed and ill-fed, staring vacantly as Leonora's coach rolled past them. Forests had been decimated, leaving nothing but acres of burned stumps, and fields lay barren of crops to be harvested. Here and there a caisson, stripped of all usable parts, lay on its side, rotting in the mud, and it seemed to Leonora that the stench of death still hung in the air, although she did not want to think too closely about the contents of the pits they passed from time to time.

By the time they had reached Ulm, even Jane had ceased her chatter of the new waltz to be danced in Vienna, and all the handsome Russian princes she would flirt with at the legation.

The inn in which they passed the night at Ulm was far better than any of the others where they had lain, but still the sheets were damp and ragged and they had to make their dinner of a bit of sausage and onions, washed down with watery beer, and nowhere did they see a male over thirteen or under seventy, unless he was missing an eye or a limb.

In the morning, René held a conversation in German with the suspicious landlord, and when he climbed into the carriage, his usually cheerful face was pale and drawn.

"What did you find to say to him?" Leonora asked.

René made a grimace. "The water between here and Linz is unfit to drink. Cholera—from which reasons, you may well guess. The Germans were unwilling to bury the French dead. He said a year ago the bodies were piled up along the road like . . . Pardon, madame! I shall say no more, but should any of you become thirsty, I would suggest you try the beer."

Strawbridge went quite white about the lips

and Leonora thought she would faint, but instead that indispensable female produced a sulfur powder and camphor, engaging herself in making up small cloth bags for each of them to wear about their necks for the next leg of the journey. "It is not at all what one is used to," she murmured from time to time, stitching away busily.

To pass the time and to distract them from the landscape, René read aloud from a guidebook to Vienna he had managed to procure somewhere near Dijon, translating it into English as he read in his light, quick voice.

" 'While possessed of neither the size nor the style of Paris or London, Vienna is nonetheless a charming city. At its center is the Hofburg, the imperial residence inhabited by his gracious majesty the Emperor Franz and his consort, Empress Louise. The Hofburg was built in the fifteenth century and has been added to considerably since, offering a variety of architectural styles that are quite impressive. . . .' "

"The host and hostess of the Congress," Jane said dreamily, huddling deeper into her pelisse, as if already seeing herself curtsying to their majesties.

To keep from looking out the window, Leonora wrapped her gloved fingers into her lap and listened to the story of Vienna's occupation by the Turks until 1683. She heard about the coffeehouses and the pastries for which the city was famous. She listened to the descriptions of the theaters and the cafés, the horse-chestnut trees that bloomed pink and white, and the varied palaces of the aristocracy, until the rocking of the coach lulled her into an uneasy and dreaming slumber.

Almost a week's traveling, together with unaccustomed discomforts and an unending landscape of nightmares, had sorely fatigued her.

Whatever Vienna was, it would certainly be better than this journey, she thought.

When the coach ground suddenly to a halt, she thought that they had reached an inn, and did not open her eyes until she heard Strawbridge screaming and René cursing volubly in French.

It was halfway to twilight and as she opened her eyes, for a moment she thought that she was seeing ghosts, for a ragged and unkempt French soldier seemed to be dragging René out of the carriage, a pistol held against his head.

Beyond this wraith, she could see other soldiers, equally ragged and wild-looking, some on horseback, some on foot, dragging the coachman down from his box and kicking him savagely with booted feet.

René was putting up a good fight, but now a second soldier had joined the first and was roughly pulling him from the box to the ground, where they pushed him, face forward, into the mud, and using the butts of their pistols, beat him about the head. There were shouts and curses, and Leonora looked quickly about her.

Strawbridge had fainted dead away, slumped in a corner of the coach against the squabs.

Jane was clearly paralyzed with terror, her

eyes wide and white, her mouth hanging slack. She had sunk back into the corner of the carriage, cowering into her pelisse.

Bandits, Leonora thought. Quickly she picked up her little muff from the corner of the carriage where it had dropped, and leaned forward to undo the latch on the carriage door on her side.

At that moment, the biggest and ugliest of the lot pulled himself through the door. Leonora's first thought was how powerfully he reeked of wine and filth as his small beady eyes darted about, looking at the three females. Strawbridge was obviously of no interest to him; Leonora received an assessing look, but it was Jane, the youngest and prettiest, upon whom he seized, grasping her arm in one enormous fist and dragging her up from her seat as if he meant to swing her over his shoulder.

"*N'assez pas*," Leonora said, surprised at how calm her voice sounded in her own ears. With her left hand she slid the tiny muff down her arm to reveal a pearl-handled pistol aimed directly at the big monster's heart.

The man looked into her eyes, and whatever he saw there must have convinced him that Leonora meant business, for he dropped the terrified Jane like a rag doll, and she crawled back into her corner of the carriage, whimpering slightly.

"I do not know if you can speak English or not," Leonora continued, using all her will to keep her voice steady, "but I know you'll understand *this*." She made a gesture with the pistol, and he took a step backward, tripping over

Strawbridge's legs and tumbling out the door.

"Quickly!" Leonora said to Jane, making for the door on her side. But Jane was immobile, and Leonora had to grasp at her arm, shaking her. "Quickly! Do you want to be raped and murdered by these savages?"

Jane struggled to her feet, and Leonora kicked open the door, just as the big soldier clambered back into the tiny box.

Leonora gave Jane a hard shove. "Run! Hide!" she commanded, facing down the big monster as he lurched toward her, cursing in French.

"So be it," Leonora said to herself, cocking the gun as he loomed directly above her. She had one shot, and she knew she had to make it count.

She pulled the trigger, and the explosion was deafening.

As she watched, the big man staggered backward, his eyes full of surprise. Red stains spread across the dirty blue tunic, and he put an enormous hand up to cover the wound. But he never made it. Still regarding Leonora with surprise, he rolled backward, looking, she thought abstractedly, like nothing so much as a hogshead rolling downhill.

Using her teeth, she opened the little chamois bag and extracted ball and powder, loading again as fast as she could.

Cursing her skirts, she backed out of the door behind her and peered about for Jane.

Darkness was gathering heavily now, and

the air was filled with the sound of men and horses.

Leonora sank ankle-deep in mud. Holding her pistol at the ready, she waited to see if Jane or any French soldier might appear, but whatever was happening, it was taking place on the other side of the carriage.

Flinging off her bonnet and shedding her sable cloak into the mud, Leonora eased herself cautiously about the boot of the coach, keeping her cover, her heart pounding in her chest.

She saw a melee of men and horses, sabers flashing as they lunged at each other desperately. Although she did not know the uniforms of the Imperial Austrian Cavalry, she knew that miraculously, a rescue party had arrived and was subduing the French soldiers, for there were men with blue uniforms bleeding into the mud at her feet.

Wildly she looked about for Jane, René, and the coachman, and, in the darkness, saw only René, leaning against a wagon wheel bleeding profusely and cursing fluently in French.

It was only then that she saw the second carriage a few yards away, and Jane seated on the step, wrapped in a familiar-looking corbeau driving cape.

She thought that she would never see a more welcome sight than the owner of that cloak, his coat slashed and torn, a wild grin on his face, and a captured saber in his hand, wheeling about as he matched his blade against that of the French leader.

"Umberto," Leonora said aloud, sinking back

against the coach to avoid being trampled by a horse.

How mad and how gay he looked to her. His mount wheeled about and he laughed, slashing at the other rider with his sword, a glitter of enjoyment in his dark eyes.

Out of the gloom, she saw the second Frenchman ride up behind Umberto, his saber raised high above that dark head. Unaware, Umberto battled on with his opponent, slashing in a broad arc at the man's tunic.

The second Frenchman started to bring his sword down toward the back of Umberto's head.

Before he could do so, Leonora had raised her pistol and fired.

With a startled look on his face, the second Frenchman slid from his horse, disappearing from her sight.

Umberto glanced at her for a single second, and his mad smile deepened, his dark eyes meeting hers in acknowledgment of her feat. He was enjoying himself, she thought wildly, dropping the pistol into her reticule. He loves the fight, the adventure of it all.

Slowly she made her way toward Jane, seating herself on the trap beside the girl, slipping an arm about her shoulders.

"We have been rescued," she said quietly, more quietly than she was feeling. "It is all over and we are safe."

Jane shivered.

6

LORD UMBERTO PICKED up the glass by its delicate stem, twirling it about in the firelight. The wine sparkled like a liquid ruby. "A band of renegade soldiers terrorizing the countryside. The last ragtag ends of Bonaparte's armies. It happens at the end of every war, I suppose. Men who cannot or will not go back to their old lives. Or perhaps that was much like their old life-style. The Imperial Cavalry has been tracking them for some time, I believe. Well, they have them now. What's left of them. Bloody savages." Cast against the blazing fire in the hearth, Umberto's profile was craggy and dark.

The warm peace of the private parlor, with the remains of a large and delicious supper still on the board, was in sharp contrast to the scene that had been enacted there only a few hours ago when Umberto had brought his ragtag charges into this old and comfortable Linz hostelry.

Leonora, viewing the world through the veil of shock, could not help but admire the way in which he had taken charge of their situation, examining the coachman for broken bones, using a piece of Strawbridge's chamois to dress René's cuts with such expertise that the doctor pronounced he could have done no better himself. Indeed, all that person declared he need do was administer sulfur powders to René and offer the hysterical Jane and Strawbridge sleeping drafts.

It seemed to Leonora that Umberto was everywhere, ordering rooms to be made up, food and drink to be served, the coach and horses to be fetched and attended to, a private parlor opened, and fires laid in all their rooms.

The staff of the inn, awed that the renegade marauders had finally been caught and were safely languishing in the dungeon of Linz Castle, fulfilled Umberto's every request as if he had been the emperor himself, with the result that the party felt amply comforted for their adventure, save for Miss Strawbridge, who, bemoaning the mud that had ruined my lady's sables, was even now lying upstairs with a cold compress on her head and a sleeping draft overtaking her overworked imagination.

Jane, stretched out upon the sofa, suppressed a genteel yawn behind her hand and drew Leonora's shawl closer about her shoulders. "I do not know what we should have done, Lord Umberto, if you had not come when you did."

That gentleman shrugged lightly. "It is more fortunate that the emperor dispatched a cavalry troop giving Wellington's equerry—myself, of course—an escort from the border to Vienna. I must say those fellows bear no great love for the French and fell to their work with gusto!"

"Even as they seem to be doing now," Leonora murmured, listening to the sounds of roistering coming from the tap.

"I did not think that outriders were necessary from Paris to Vienna," René moaned from his chair by the fire, looking very grievous indeed in all his bandages. "How can I forgive myself for such a gross oversight? *Sprasti! Je suis inconsolable, madame.*"

Leonora raised a hand in protest, but it was Umberto who spoke. "How were you to know? Communications are still very bad between the Germanies and Austria. Years of war have broken everything down. Buck up, old boy! *I* should never have thought of outriders had not the emperor provided them for me, you know, purely as a ceremonial bit."

"Umberto is quite right," Leonora put in. "René, you must not blame yourself."

"But I do!" René made to rise, and winced. No bones had been broken, but he was badly bruised from the beating he had taken.

Jane yawned again. "I think the sleeping powders are taking effect," she sighed. "I shall have no nightmares tonight."

"Then off to bed with you at once!" Umberto commanded.

Jane rose gracefully from the chaise. Crossing the room, she put her arms about Lady Leonora and gave her a hug. "I owe you both my life and my honor, dear ma'am!" she exclaimed fiercely. "If you had not saved me from that terrible man, I do not know what should have become of me."

"It was nothing, my dear," Lady Leonora replied a little gruffly, patting Jane's shoulder. "One simply learns to think on one's feet."

"I still owe you my honor and my life!" Jane declared passionately, and quite spoiled it all with yet another yawn.

"Off to bed!" Lady Leonora commanded. "And be sure that that goose Strawbridge has warmed the sheets for you!"

"I shall follow, if I may," René declared, heaving his delicate frame from the chair with a grimace of pain. *"Ce jour*—it has been *un jour malade et mauvais!"*

When they were alone, Leonora closed her eyes, holding out her glass for more wine. "Oh, Lord! This started as a journey of pleasure!" she sighed, shaking her head ruefully.

Umberto seated himself in the chair lately vacated by René and began to peel an apple with his pocketknife, tossing the peelings into the fire.

"In the West Country, where my family lives, there is a superstition that if you throw your apple peels into the fire, they will twist and turn into the initial of your sweetheart."

Leonora glanced into the flames, sipping her wine. Her hand trembled slightly, and she rested the glass on the table beside her.

"Do you know, I believe that one there, beside the andiron, is turning into an L," Umberto remarked airily.

"Silly, superstitious nonsense," Leonora said firmly, even though the shriveling peel *did* look very like an L.

There was a not unpleasant silence between them for a space of time, during which the noise from the tap turned into the slurred sounds of a drinking song.

Umberto leaned back in his chair, resting his polished boots, somewhat scarred by his recent activities, on the stool before him, and regarded Lady Leonora from beneath his thick brows.

"An interesting little pistol, ma'am. Manton, I believe?"

Leonora looked up with a startled expression. "Manton?"

"Joseph Manton and Company, Gunsmiths, London." Umberto's voice was airy. "Good man, Joseph Manton! I own several fowling pieces from his hand."

"Yes, it is a Manton. It was made especially for me. My father had a dread of highwaymen, you see, and he presented me with this pair. I have always thought it prudent to travel with one of them in my muff and the other in my portmanteau."

"And I see that you know how to use it."

"Well enough. But I have never used it against a human being before."

Suddenly she rose and crossed the room, fumbling in her reticule. "This is it. I do not think that I want it anymore. Perhaps you would like to keep it as a souvenir of an interesting evening. I do not think that I want to see it anymore."

She tossed the little gun across the room, and Umberto caught it expertly in his hand.

"A fine little piece. It fires, I should think, a little to the right, but . . ."

Leonora had turned toward the window, her shoulders shaking.

Umberto crossed the room, placing a comforting arm about her shoulders. "Go ahead and have a good cry. I always find that it makes one feel a great deal better," he said gently.

"Or a very great fool!" Leonora exclaimed, searching her reticule for a handkerchief. "Above all things I dislike females who make watering pots of themselves!"

She blew her nose.

"I would think that a lady who has endured a great deal of adventure would have a perfect right to cry," Umberto said.

"Too much adventure!" Leonora exclaimed. "Rape and murder are too much adventure."

"I might remind you that you were neither raped nor murdered. I was always told that if you came out of it alive and relatively unharmed, then you might call it an adventure."

Leonora gave him a sideways glance, biting her lower lip. "Umberto, you are *impossible!*" she announced.

"Oh yes, I know," he responded airily. "But I am very charming also, you know."

"You *reek* of charm, of course!" Leonora exclaimed, desperately attempting to keep her lips from trembling, whether from laughter or utter frustration, she was unable to tell.

But he looked so innocent that she was forced to conceal her smile with a handkerchief, shaking her head. "Impossible man!" she repeated firmly.

"Oh, very much so," he said gravely. "I am odious, overbearing, far too encroaching for my own good, and probably a good many other things."

"But *full* of charm!" Leonora said, allowing herself to be coaxed little by little out of herself.

"I have been told that I *reek* of it!" Umberto declared, shaking his head soulfully. "Rather as if it were a strong cologne."

"If it were, then half the men in London would be splashing themselves with it," Leonora chuckled.

"*That* would be something to witness. Fortunately, it is a quality possessed by a mere fortunate few, and we must be modest in our use of it."

"Oh, most definitely, for charm can be so devastating," Leonora replied quickly. "How much, how very much you seemed to be enjoying yourself out there, in the thick of the fray," she observed, suddenly serious.

Umberto shrugged. "I suppose that I was. By God, it was like being back in the Peninsula again, fighting with Old Hook. There *was* adventure, by Jove! We'd ride through mud and blood up to our saddle girths all day and all night, sleeping on our horses, bivouacking in little Spanish towns . . . *There* was a time! The only thing better was Brazil!"

"You were there also?"

"Oh, yes! An ill-fated thing that was, and I had goal fever on top of it all, but I came out all right and tight in the end, so there's the difference."

"It must be from being christened Umberto," Leonora remarked.

"Eh?" he said, a little startled.

"Well, Umberto was the hero of a novel, very popular in our mothers' day, about a swashbuckling sort, a pirate, who had a great many adventures of all kinds."

"You may be right, you know. When I was born, there was a fashion for all things Italian, and I always assumed that my parents had chosen my name for that reason. But even when I was a little boy, I wanted to have . . . adventures. Wanted to be a pirate on the Spanish Main with a dagger in my teeth and the Skull and Crossbones flying from the main!"

"I can well picture that," Leonora said thoughtfully.

"I was a terrible brat, I fear, and drove my nanny and my governesses to distraction until I went to Harrow."

"One may well imagine that," Leonora said. "And I suppose they beat all of that out of you at Harrow?"

"Rather the contrary! I became even more determined to have adventures. And I had some, too. I once tried to run away to sea. As a cabin boy on an India merchantman."

"And I suppose you were sent down from Cambridge for having adventures?"

"Oxford, and yes, I was rusticated for having a very peculiar adventure. That's when I bought my colors and went out to Brazil."

"You must find it very dull to be in the diplomatic corps, Umberto."

"Oh, one still manages to have adventures here and there, you know," Umberto said. "But tell me about you. Persons of charm, you know, do not always talk of themselves. They listen to others, which makes others believe them charming."

"Perhaps so. But of me, there is little to tell. I was a very dull little girl, I fear, whose greatest adventures were walks in the park with my governess. If you want adventure, I think you should talk to Miss Hobart, for I imagine her destiny is a great many adventures."

"I think you are correct there. But surely, even as you walked through the park sedately with your governess, you thought of faraway places and other life-styles?"

"I read a great many novels from the Minerva Press, and fancied myself a great heroine."

"Which, of course, you had to hide from your governess, and only read by candlelight after the lights were gone down."

"On the contrary, Addy—Miss Addington, my governess—and I were both great readers of the Minerva Press Novels. We used to walk to the village posting station in town to intercept them from my parents and my brothers. Poor Addy! I wonder how she goes on, saddled with those brats of my brother's! Oh, all my adventures were led in the imagination, you see, but such an imagination I had!" Lady Leonora chuckled. "I fancied myself a *terrific* heroine and went about striking attitudes that my brothers would mock. I was a dreadful little girl!"

"On the contrary, you sound very dulcet to me, my lady! One could almost wish one had known you."

She sighed. "Oh, I am certain that you would have taken an instant and violent dislike to me. I was a great silly, and very *stoopid* and utterly in love with Lord Byron!"

"You must have been quite the little romantic."

"Oh yes! I was a great romantic, you know, fancying this and that and all the rest, until I was married."

"Until you were married," Umberto repeated, and it was as if a pall had been cast over the room, both of them recalling the painful circumstances of her widowhood.

"Marriage, Lord Umberto, disabused me of all romantic notions," Leonora said dryly, taking a pace about the room, allowing his arm to fall away from her shoulders. "At least a marriage to Richard. I think it would have disabused the most naive female of any romantic notions of love and marriage."

"Perhaps I may speak frankly, since we seem to be confiding in one another, Lady Leonora?" Umberto said gently, leaning against the arm of the Windsor chair and watching her pacing the room, her face impassive, unreadable in the firelight. "From what I know of Dick, and I knew him long, and not always, as you know, in the most pleasant circumstances, I would ask that you judge neither love nor marriage by your experiences with him."

Leonora glanced at him over her shoulder. "Ah, sir! But those are the only circumstances by which I might judge. Hardly, as you say, the most pleasant, but enough to make me vow that I have no heart."

"I have heard that said of you, my lady, but something forbids me to believe it," Umberto said quite seriously, frowning at her and thrusting his hands in his pockets. "A person without heart does not go about rescuing Bath misses in French inns, and delivering them all the way across Europe to their papas in Vienna."

"There! The merest trifle, I assure you!" Lady Leonora said with a toss of her head. "Besides, Jane is different! I have become quite fond of her, in a way, and one—"

"And one proves, against one's own inclinations, that one has a heart!" Umberto concluded triumphantly.

"Piffle," Lady Leonora said firmly, but two small pink spots burned in her cheeks.

"And one might further surmise that if my lady were inclined to adopt Bath misses in distress, and émigrés in need of employment, and heaven only knows what else, that my lady might also become susceptible to the more tender emotions connected with love."

"The grandest piffle," Leonora said firmly. "One has no heart, you must recall!"

"Ah, but what if one chose to believe otherwise? Suppose, beneath that wounded exterior, that romantic girl still might exist?"

"She has been quite extinguished." Leonora peered in the mirror and patted her curls with trembling hands. "The entire idea is utterly impossible."

"I wonder," Umberto said thoughtfully.

In the morning, over a hearty Austrian breakfast featuring many varieties of sausage and pastries and coffee, during which my lady Leonora and my lord Umberto treated each other with frigid politeness, plans were made to complete the trip to Vienna.

Lady Leonora's coachman was in no shape to travel, having sustained several broken ribs, and it was decided that he would be left at the inn to recuperate in the care of the staff, who never seemed to tire of hearing about his part in the capture of the dreadful French marauders. When the doctor pronounced him recovered, he would bring the coach from Linz to Vienna.

Leonora and Umberto were not the only persons somewhat the worse for wear after the previous evening. René toyed alternately with his breakfast and a hand mirror in which he bemoaned the temporary disfigurement of his countenance.

Jane, dark circles under her eyes, seemed nonetheless to have sustained her appetite, for she devoured a great many sausages, and so many tortes and pastries that Lady Leonora wondered if she was possessed of a hollow leg.

Oblivious of the tensions between Umberto and Leonora, she and René chattered away, arguing amiably about who would be permitted to ride in the box of Umberto's carriage, since it was decided they would all enter the city in that conveyance.

Miss Strawbridge stuck her head in the door to dourly remind my lady that not all of her trunks and bandboxes could possibly be expected to fit into Lord Umberto's vehicle.

It was well past ten when Lady Leonora's wardrobe had been restructured, the coachman provided for, René's bandages attended to, Strawbridge settled with her camphor bags and sulfur packets and a thankful farewell bid to the Imperial and very blue-deviled Cavalry officers.

Leonora was glad that Umberto chose to ride on the box with his driver. She did not think she could have borne to be in an enclosed space with him for the space of a long day. It was bad enough, she discovered, to have to endure the chatter of Jane and René as they bickered over a traveling cribbage board, and the muttered imprecations of Strawbridge recalling she had left my lady's very best cashmere shawl with the coach.

Indeed, it was almost a relief when they stopped at a posting inn for luncheon and she was able to sit at a charming and rustic table beneath a linden tree instead of a lurching carriage.

She was surprised when Umberto approached her, and without a word, produced an orange from his pocket, winking most rougishly as he handed it to her.

"Thank you," Leonora said, truly grateful.

"It was nothing. Best you let me peel it for you, though," Umberto said, easing his long legs over the bench as he leaned against the tree and began to use his penknife to expose the succulent fruit beneath the skin.

Leonora ate it section by section, savoring the sweet juicy pulp.

"In the West Country, we have a trick with orange pips. You count the number of them, and that will tell you how long it will be before your sweetheart comes," he remarked lazily.

Before Leonora could make a reply, there was a thunder of hoofbeats, and a liveried rider drew up in the inn yard.

"My lord Umberto!" he cried, rushing across the grass. "Dispatches from Paris, sir."

Reluctantly Umberto rose to his feet, taking the black case from the messenger. "Yes, of course," he sighed. "Come into the inn."

Leonora stared after him. If the truth were to be told, she suddenly felt just a trifle vexed.

In spite of herself, she began to count the orange pips in her hand.

7

EVEN THOUGH NIGHT had fallen before they reached Vienna, it seemed to Leonora as if the city was bathed in light, for almost every building and house seemed to be illuminated from within, as if everyone in the city were giving a party. Despite the lateness of the hour, people of all classes and conditions strolled the streets, taking the fine autumn air. Every square and corner seemed to be possessed of a park, for there were more trees and lawns than she had seen in any other city. Even the architecture, baroque and fanciful, seemed to give the city a festive air, as if it were a sort of fairyland. The very air seemed to smell of romance and intrigue, and from time to time she heard snatches of music as if to set all the world dancing.

Her heart lifted, for no reason at all, save the joy of being alive.

The carriage pulled up before a small baroque town house, and Jane leaned across Leonora to look out the window. "Oh, my lady! This is Papa's house!" she exclaimed.

"It is indeed your papa's house," Umberto said. Having leapt down from the box, he opened the door to assist them to descend.

Without waiting, Jane rushed ahead of them and up the stairs, where she pounded on the big iron knocker, hopping in a most unladylike manner from one foot to the other.

Strawbridge muttered from the depths of the carriage.

The door was opened by a funereal-looking personage who stood and blinked for several seconds at the unexpected sight of a Bath miss on the doorstep.

"Ah, Chandler!" Jane said gaily. "It is I—or is it me? How are you? Is Papa at home? I have come such a long way and had a great many adventures!"

The funereal person's face suddenly broke into a smile as brilliant as it was unexpected. "Miss Jane! By heaven, it *is* you, miss!"

"Of course it is me, Chandler, and very glad to be here, too! And I have brought several people with me who are cold and tired and hungry, so would you fetch Papa and tell him?"

The butler recollected himself. "Yes, miss, of course. Sir Julian is dressing for dinner, so if you would be good enough to allow the footman to take you and your friends into the Yellow Saloon . . ." The sight of a nattily dressed gentleman, a fashionable lady, a wraithlike young man covered in sticking plasters, and a haughty abigail clutching a jewel case against her withered bosom seemed to reassure him somewhat, but he still shook his head in a manner Strawbridge approved as he trod up the steps.

The Austrian footman, whose English was limited, led the way to the Yellow Saloon, standing back respectfully as they all trooped in.

The footman immediately started to light more tapers, illuminating this chamber into a fuller brightness.

It would have been better had he not, for it was quite the most hideous room Leonora had ever seen, full of heavy, ornately carved seventeenth-century furniture cushioned in a particularly nightmarish shade of ocher damask. It seemed that every available surface was covered with ornamental bric-a-brac in a bewildering variety of periods and styles, and the walls, also painted a vile yellow where the plaster was not falling away from the lathing, were mercifully covered with a great many tapestries depicting, in a rather graphic manner, the various martyrdoms of several of the more minor saints.

"Good God," Lady Leonora said simply.

Jane, already making herself at home by removing her bonnet and pelisse, looked about and made a most unladylike face. "Poor Papa," she said simply. "It is not at all like our house in Upper Mount Street."

René, picking up and examining a Turkish cloisonné vase, shook his head.

Strawbridge clutched Lady Leonora's jewel case all the harder and glared at the puzzled Austrian footman, who stood awaiting orders.

"The accommodations in Vienna are so scarce that we all take whatever we can get," Umberto said, pushing his hands into his pockets and frowning at a St. Sebastian in particularly bad taste. "Over at the Minoriztenplatz, I share an attic room with a junior attaché. It has rats."

"I would not be surprised if there were rats here," Jane said matter-of-factly, turning the edge of a mildewed carpet with her toe. "Poor Papa. I think it has been difficult for him since Mama died."

"There is no need to make it more so by enduring a decor *comme ça*," René murmured.

"Jane! By all that's holy!"

All of them turned at once as a tall man strode into the room, still attired in his dressing gown. His resemblance to his daughter announced him to be Sir Julian Hobart. He was fair, with high cheekbones and a hairline that was beginning to recede slightly from a finely shaped forehead. Although his expression was, at the moment, forbidding, there was more than a trace of humor in his blue eyes, and his wide, thin lips twitched as he beheld his only offspring.

"Papa!" Jane cried, and threw herself against the heavy Chinese embroidery of his dressing gown. "Oh, Papa, what adventures I have had!"

Sir Julian embraced his daughter almost fiercely, before holding her away from himself at arm's length to survey her from head to toe. "Do you wish to see your pater stick his spoon in the wall before the age of forty-five, girl? Chandler never gave me such a turn as when he announced that you were here! Why are you not at Miss Gunnerston's, and how did you come to Vienna?"

Suddenly Sir Julian became aware of the presence of others in the room, and still holding Jane, surveyed them all, greatly puzzled.

"Hullo, Umberto, old man. Heard you were coming from Paris, but how do you come to be mixed up with this minx of a daughter of mine, and who will make me acquainted with the rest of you?"

"Hobart, my good man, I see I find you well," drawled Umberto. "I simply come to provide escort for the lady who has undertaken to restore your daughter to you. Lady Leonora Ware, may I present Sir Julian Hobart?"

Sir Julian thrust out his hand, holding Leonora's just a shade longer than necessary. She was aware that he found her attractive, and was not unflattered. "The pleasure is mine, I assure you, madam. I only hope that this silly chit has not put you through a great many troubles."

Leonora smiled fondly at Jane. "We have had adventures, sir, but as you can see, we have arrived safely."

"Lady Leonora is the most complete hand, Papa," Jane gushed. "When we were set upon by bandits, she drew her little pistol and—"

Umberto cleared his throat. "And may I also present M. le Comte D'Aubusson, Lady Leonora's *cicerone*. And of course, Miss Strawbridge, Lady Leonora's abigail.

"It is not at all what an Englishwoman is used to," muttered Strawbridge.

"No, I rather think not," Sir Julian mused,

turning to his daughter again. "But why are you not at Miss Gunnerston's?"

"This, I believe, is where I exit, stage left," Umberto murmured airily, picking up his hat. "Dispatches. Have to go immediately to the Minoriztenplatz. Charlie Stewart's waiting, and you know what *he's* like. Lady Leonora, Miss Hobart, hope you will allow me to call on you to see how you do. Hobart, tomorrow morning in Castlereagh's office?"

"Of course, old man, of course. Forgive me if I am not a good host, but it is not every day that one's daughter appears unexpectedly on one's doorstep damn near two thousand miles from where she's supposed to be, what?"

"I quite understand," Umberto agreed, nodding to René and Miss Strawbridge. "No bother, old man, I can find my way to the door," he told the bemused Austrian footman.

"And perhaps you could direct us to a good hotel," Lady Leonora added after the door had closed behind Umberto.

"Oh, no, you must stay with us!" Jane protested. "Please, Lady Leonora! There are to be parties and balls and all manner of entertainment, and it would be nothing without *you*! Cannot Lady Leonora stay, Papa? She brought me all the way from Calais to here, and quite ruined her own plans, all for my sake!"

"I'm sorry, Jane, but even if your papa were to agree, which I am certain he would not wish to do, it would be quite improper for me to stay in a household without a hostess."

Jane shook her curls. "But *I* am your hostess,

Lady Leonora! It don't signify that I'm not quite
out yet, does it, Papa?" Suddenly her eyes were
alight. "Anyway, Lady Leonora might bring me
out, you know!"

Sir Julian looked so thoroughly adrift that
it was all Leonora could do not to laugh aloud.
"If you would be kind enough, Sir Julian to
direct us to a good hotel, I think that would be
quite enough," she said firmly, feeling that
gentleman was going to have quite enough upon
his plate when Jane told her whole story.

But Sir Julian shook his head. "Nonsense.
This house is no palace, but it will easily accommodate four more persons. My dear Lady Leonora, you could not find a doss house in this city
with a bed to spare. This is a city of two hundred
thousand souls, and I am given to understand
that another two hundred thousand have crowded
in for the Congress. It is evident to me that you
have rescued my foolish daughter from the
consequences of her own folly. The least I might
be permitted to do is give you food and shelter
and entertainment during your stay here." As
he spoke, he wrapped his arm about Jane's
shoulders and smiled so openly and sincerely at
Leonora that she hesitated.

"As to propriety, ma'am, this is Europe, not
England, and things are looked upon very dif-
ferently here. I think Jane makes an excellent
chaperon."

"I shall be certain that we all behave with
the utmost propriety," Miss Hobart laughed.
"We shall be very dull indeed. Oh, Lady Leonora,
please, please do stay with us!"

How to resist such a charming father and daughter?

"I would be honored," Leonora replied.

"Oh, this is famous above all things!" Jane exclaimed.

The look in Sir Julian's eyes made Leonora realize that he agreed.

At that moment, with a discreet clearing of the throat, Chandler appeared in the doorway. "Excuse me, sir. Anticipating your orders, I have taken the liberty of placing my lady's trunks in the Flower Room. My lady's abigail's things will be found in the adjoining dressing room, and my lady's majordomo's articles I have placed in the red chamber. Miss Jane, I hope you will be happy to be in the Egyptian Room. It is next to Sir Julian's apartments. Also, sir, I have taken the liberty of sending a footman around to Princess Bagration's, informing her of the circumstances which make it impossible to dine with her tonight." Again he cleared his throat. "Also, I have ordered a dinner to be served in the small dining room at your convenience. Is an hour sufficient, sir?"

Leonora, startled, looked at Jane. "Chandler always knows what you want before you do," the young girl whispered. "Papa says he is worth his weight in gold if only for that one talent."

Leonora could only agree.

An hour later, she left Strawbridge's capable hands bathed, refreshed, and becomingly attired in a dinner dress of claret-colored watered silk, with a deep décolleté trimmed with a row of blond lace in Vandyke points and a rouleau of white satin banding the high waist. The wadded hem was trimmed with corsages of the same white satin, and deeply hemmed in Vandyke points of the same blond lace. Upon her feet she wore satin slippers with claret scallops at the toe, and she carried a shawl of gossamer silver spiderweb gauze over one arm. Strawbridge had dressed her hair *à la russe,* threading her dark curls with satin ribbon and pearls, and if just a touch of rouge had been applied to her cheeks, well, it was a secret between mistress and maid. About Leonora's neck she had clasped a pearl-and-diamond lavalière, and baroque pearls depended from both her ears. Long kid gloves covered her arms, and upon one wrist she wore a diamond-and-pearl bracelet.

As she descended the staircase, Sir Julian, who stood waiting below, recognized her as a female who was every inch the fashionable lady and nodded to himself with satisfaction.

He was not badly turned out, he knew. He had excellent legs and looked well in knee breeches. His waistcoat was of a simple gray and white stripe, and he wore only a single fob on his watch, the Imperial Seal of Russia, a gift from the czar. His charcoal-gray evening coat was cut to perfection, and his cravat, knotted into the style known as the Sophisticate, was both elegant and simple.

"Allow me to tell you how very much in the first style you look, Lady Leonora," he said, offering her his arm at the foot of the stairs. "That red is vastly becoming to you."

She smiled, for no one can resist a compliment, and Leonora loved her clothes.

"I fear Jane will take a little time dressing, for she and I had a little talk while you were refreshing yourself. I had no idea that that Gunnerston woman ran such a school . . ."

"She did when I was there," Leonora said as they passed through the arched hallway into a smaller but no less hideous salon done up in the gilt-and-brocade decor of Maria Theresa's reign.

Seeing Leonora wince, Sir Julian laughed. "By God, ma'am, it is dreadful, ain't it? Start to wonder what the devil the owners were thinking about. But if I told you the rent the legation's paying for it, you'd understand why Baron and Baroness von Whatever are off on their estates laughing."

But a cheerful fire burned in the marble fireplace, and Chandler had placed decanters of Madeira and sherry on a table.

Leonora sat down in a deceptively comfortable-looking armchair by the hearth and sipped gratefully the glass of sherry Sir Julian handed her. Having poured himself some Madeira, Sir Julian sat down opposite her, crossing one well-formed leg over the other. "We drink out of glasses in the shape of dolphins," he remarked absently. "Or are they slugs? You never know around here what something is supposed to be."

Leonora held the crystal up to the light, frowning doubtfully. "I should be tempted to say hedgehogs," she concluded at last.

"Well, madam," Sir Julian started suddenly,

"I find myself greatly in your debt. From what little I know of you, and from what Jane has told me, I believe you are a female of great courage and common sense. And great generosity. To bring a chit of a girl like my Jane all the way across Europe—"

"Please, Sir Julian. I am quite fond of Jane, and one simply does what one has to."

"You are far too modest, Lady Leonora!" Sir Julian protested. "Far too modest by half, ma'am! For, still and all, I find myself deeply in debt to you. Jane is my only child, you know. Charlotte—my wife—died in childbirth with our second child, and since then Jane is all that I've had. Can't say that I don't love her, because I do, although I'm more than just angry with her for this escapade she's pulled!"

"If you had been unfortunate enough to attend that Gunnerston harpy's school, Sir Julian, I do not doubt that you would have done the same. I know that I yearned to. Indeed, had there been a place for me to go, I would have gone."

"So you say. So you say, and I cannot doubt it. But how was I to know? I thought she would be well taken care of there. Apparently I was wrong. But Jane never was one to hold the bridle when she could run wild."

"No, I think not," Lady Leonora replied. "She is a very high-spirited girl. If you will permit me to say so, Sir Julian, I think it is time that she was out. It will give her greater freedom, and at the same time, it will keep her so occupied that she will have no need to think up new adventures for herself."

A look of vast relief crossed Sir Julian's face. "Exactly so, Lady Leonora, exactly so! And what better place to bring her out than Vienna? Town's packed with eligible young Englishmen lookin' for wives! You don't know what it's like, ma'am! Parties, balls, dances, fetes, routs—and the Congress ain't even open yet! She'll meet more men here than she'd meet at Almack's in three seasons!"

"Yes, I suppose so," Lady Leonora agreed. "Surely there must be several ladies at the legation who would be willing to sponsor her."

Sir Julian twisted his glass about in his hands, looking down at the floor. He cleared his throat once or twice and then stood up, leaning carelessly against the mantelpiece, dislodging a porcelain shepherdess from her precarious position beside an ormolu clock. "Thing of it is, Lady Leonora, I spend all day and half my night mincing words. That's diplomacy, you know, mincing words, like a dancing master minces steps! Thing of it is, what Jane wants, I like to give her, and she's set her heart on your bringing her out here in Vienna. There! The long and the short of it."

Leonora sat speechless, quite certain that her mouth was hanging open. "I?" she asked incredulously.

"Yes, ma'am. You, if you would be so good and kind. It would mean a great deal to Jane, you know. She thinks the world of you, Lady

Leonora. And I . . . well, I'm coming to hold you in pretty high esteem myself!"

"But I am not at all political, have never moved in political circles, know no one in political circles, and have never brought anyone out in my life!"

Sir Julian shrugged all these objections off lightly. "My secretary will give you the list of people you'll want to invite. There is a ballroom here, although, Lord knows, it's a dismal-looking place. I think the walls drip. Of course, you can have carte blanche to spend just as much as you like. Buy yourself a few fripperies, too, while you're at it."

Now Leonora had to laugh aloud. "My dear Sir Julian, if you knew me better you would know that I am the most selfish creature alive, and care only for my own comfort. It is true that I have become fond of Jane, but that, I assure you, is purely a *fluke*. Aside from which, I have an extremely warm income and have no need to allow other persons to purchase my fripperies, as you call them! Besides, I was thinking that in a day or two, I might travel on to Sardinia and Greece!"

"Both of them dead bores, you know. Hot, dirty, and full of revolutionaries." Thus Sir Julian dismissed Sardinia and Greece. "Vienna, Lady Leonora, is where everyone shall be this season."

"Perhaps too many people. One too many people," Leonora murmured to herself.

" 'Tother thing," Sir Julian added, running a finger around the neck of his shirt. "Vienna's full of attractive females, Lady Leonora. Now, you and I are persons of the world, and damn, well, a man's not a *monk*, you know. Might even think of getting married again and settling down. Thing of it is, wife might not like Jane, nor Jane a wife. If she were settled in her own home, with a husband, so much the better for both of us."

"Have you anyone in mind?" Leonora asked curiously.

"No, but I have been looking about, you know." Sir Julian thrust his hands into his pockets, looking as if he wanted to blush. "Damn, madam, I hate to ask you for anything else, after what you've done for my Jane so far, but she says it's Lady Leonora or no one, and so it must be."

"But surely, Lady Castlereagh, or Lady Burghesh—"

"Emily Castlereagh's a walking cipher! She appeared at a fancy-dress ball in a bedsheet, wearing Castlereagh's Order of the Garter as a hair ornament!"

"I suppose she is a trifle eccentric," Lady Leonora admitted. "But a very kind soul."

"Of Priscilla Burghesh, the less said the better. Besides, she is only twenty-two, and hardly has established the credit to bring out a young girl into society."

"Oh, dear," Leonora murmured.

"Lastly, madam, I need you. Were I to have a hostess to preside over my table, I should be able to entertain some of the most important and powerful men and women in Europe. And who knows what might be accomplished over a sherry trifle or a rack of veal?"

"You make jokes!" Leonora said, shaking her head.

"On the contrary, Lady Leonora, I am quite serious," Sir Julian answered, refilling her glass. "You see, it is far more I ask of you than to merely chaperon Jane from one event to another."

"Far more indeed," said a lazy voice from the doorway, and Leonora turned to see Umberto, in impeccable evening dress of his usual black hue, smiling lazily at her as he took in her costume with an approving eye.

"Ah, Umberto, come in. I have been hoping for your voice to add to my own here," Sir Julian said.

"We shall make a chorus," Lord Umberto drawled as he crossed the room and helped himself to sherry. "What shall we drink to? To Lady Leonora?"

Thoroughly puzzled, Leonora looked from one man to the other, but could read nothing but seriousness in their expressions.

"Perhaps you would like to sit down, Leonora," Umberto suggested, and in a daze, she did as he requested.

Umberto ranged himself against the back of a settee, holding his glass in both hands. Sir Julian continued to lean against the fireplace, watching them both with sharp blue eyes that missed nothing.

"Understand, Lady Leonora," Umberto began slowly and carefully. "Vienna exists in a constant broil of intrigue and scandal. Perhaps it always has. Maria Theresa established a secret police to go about and snoop into the private affairs of its citizens, and Franz has continued the practice. I would not doubt that even now that rather unappealing footman is reporting the presence of you, Jane, and your entourage to the powers that be. It simply is, and one learns to accept it as a rather laughable and inefficient spy system. Just one among many, actually. But scandal and gossip are the meat and drink here. The choice of a man's mistress may well affect the outcome of a border dispute, for as much politicking occurs in bedrooms and ballrooms as there are assignations and billets-doux flying through the conference rooms."

Sir Julian shook his head. "At the legation, we all think it's a bit of a go, of course, but beneath all the fun and games, there is a great deal of serious work being carried on."

"The future of Europe," Umberto picked up, "is being determined right now. And, should you stay, you will be not only a witness to it, but perhaps a part. A vital part."

Sir Julian drained his glass. "It is not just that bringing out a green girl in an atmosphere such as this requires the talents of a lady such as yourself, with vast social experience and a shrewd judgment for who and what will or will not do, you know." He cleared his throat. "There is far more to it than that."

"You would, of course, be acting as Sir Julian's hostess. And a very charming hostess I know you will be," Umberto stated with a smile.

"But also, acting as my hostess, you would be presiding over a table that would include some of the greatest and most powerful people in Europe. And you would be invited to gatherings where these people were present."

"And of course, you would hear much gossip and conversation that would be of great value to our legation." Umberto's dark eyes met hers.

Lady Leonora rose from her chair and paced the length of the room, turning the stem of her glass in her hand. "Good God! You make me sound as if I were an adventuress!" she finally exclaimed, whirling to face them both.

"No more an adventuress than a grand duchess of Russia, a dozen princesses, several lesser duchesses, a covey of countesses, and a bevy of baronesses," Umberto said lightly. "It is all the crack to collect information, you know."

"It sounds perfectly dreadful to me," Leonora replied, glaring at him. "Are you asking me to snoop into people's desks and reticules like a maid?"

"Of course not, my dear Lady Leonora!" Sir Julian said, much offended. "We have other persons to do that sort of work, and they are very highly trained, at that!"

"No, we do not ask you to do anything that would jeopardize your person," Umberto agreed. "You're just not trained for it. A great shame, that. You would have done very well purloining papers, disguised as a maid."

The flush in Leonora's cheeks needed no rouge. "You are *very* odious, Umberto."

He shrugged. "As you will."

"Madam, for our purposes, you are perfect. Your social position in London is impeccable. By birth, you are from one of the oldest families in the country, and by your late marriage you are connected into one of the warmest fortunes. You have style, grace, wit, and charm, all most valuable assets. And of course, your position as a beautiful widow does you no harm, either," Sir Julian said.

"But exactly what is my position?" Leonora asked. "Am I to creep about ballrooms eavesdropping on people's assignations and intrigues?"

"One hopes you would be a little more subtle than that," Umberto said lazily.

"No, nothing so obvious. We would simply like you to allow people to confide in you. It's very simple really. One only need to be a good listener and all manner of things come pouring out," Sir Julian said.

"Exercise that legendary charm. Be gracious and interested. And remember all you hear. That is all you really need do," Umberto pronounced.

"You have laid me out a full plate, gentlemen!" Leonora said. "I am to bring out a young girl, become Sir Julian's hostess, and spy on everyone in sight!"

"Something like," Sir Julian said affably.

"Of course, everyone will be spying on you, too," Umberto added. "Everyone spies on everyone else. That's why this is all such a great go!"

"There you all are!" Jane, simply attired in white muslin and a single string of pearls, appeared in the doorway. "I'm utterly famished and Chandler is waiting to serve dinner. Papa, will you give me your arm?"

Umberto offered his to Leonora. "So, what say you?" he asked in a low voice.

"In for a penny, in for a pound. But I warn you, if there's the least trouble, Umberto—"

"Oh, there won't be! I promise you that!"

8

STRAWBRIDGE, HAVING DEPOSITED Lady Leonora's morning chocolate and croissant upon her lap, remarked dourly that she had not closed her eyes all night for the sheer monstrosity of the decor of her room.

"And this is even worse, my lady! Them nekkid gold babies hangin' all over the ceiling, doing heathen things! How you can be standing it, I don't know, for it's not what a good Englishwoman is used to seein'!"

Leonora, with a mouth full of croissant, peered above her nightcap at the carved ceiling and agreed that it was not at all what a good Englishwoman should be used to. When she suggested that it appeared to her to be more suitable to a place like a house of ill repute, Strawbridge sniffed disapprovingly and piously demanded to know what my lady would choose to wear that morning.

This question was soon settled by the appearance of Jane, full of the announcement that her Papa had given her carte blanche to purchase as many clothes as she liked, provided Lady Leonora would assist in the selection.

She was further full of the information that all the very best modistes of Paris had descended upon Vienna en masse, no doubt attracted by the clatter of so much aristocratic gold assembled in one place. That Jane seemed to have procured this information from her father made Leonora slightly suspicious about the sort of female with whom he had been consorting.

Nonetheless, after having assured herself that René was well occupied in ordering the Viennese footmen to rearrange the main salons to his taste, with already beneficial results, Leonora and Jane set off in Sir Julian's barouche, ready to be guided by the jovial Viennese coachman to the establishment of one Madame Celeste, a modiste well known to Lady Leonora from London.

Indeed, Madame Celeste recalled so excellent a client as Lady Leonora Ware quite well, and all of her sharklike teeth were exposed as she abandoned a German princess to a minion and sailed, man-o'-war-like, across the shop to greet my lady with effusion.

Having decided that Jane's case was far worse than her own, Leonora immediately turned her over to the good offices of Madame.

Dresses there must be, for a debutante has many functions to attend, and Madame Celeste had not accumulated her considerable fortune by stinting on a young girl about to make her come-out. There was a morning dress of ivory muslin, richly trimmed in Brussels lace and satin ribbons; there was a morning dress of sprigged India muslin ruched with pointe-de-Venise lace and lozenge satin; there was a walking dress of celestial blue with rose sarcenet *bords anglaises* and a ruff of scalloped corsages; there was an afternoon dress in straw yellow, high neck and long sleeves trimmed in canary georgette with a banded hem caught with corsages of ivy satin. There had to be a new pelisse, of course, of pastel aquamarine trimmed with ermine. A riding habit of bottle-green broadcloth cut *à la militaire* with epaulets and frogged closings. An evening dress of silver webbed gauze over white silk, trimmed with embroideries of ivy, and another of rose peau-de-soie, the banded hem wadded with lozenges of deeper rose, and the bodice covered with silk netting. That the merest of these confections would set Sir Julian back three hundred guineas bothered neither Lady Leonora nor Jane, and having ordered them, they set to work with Madame Celeste to design Jane's ball dress for her come-out.

Leonora herself chose only a few things. A ball gown of pomona-green crepe over a slip of threaded lamé silk hemmed with rouleaux and corsages of eau-de-Nil, a walking dress of fawn-colored gros-de-Naples, with a scrolled front and a pelerine with a dropped ceinture, and a geranium-red round dress banded with corded straw-colored satin. These, she thought, would do nicely while she was waiting for her trunks to arrive from Linz.

But she found that she could not resist a Persian shawl of varying shades of wine, particularly after Madame Celeste discovered an error in the price, and generously allowed Lady Leonora to have it for only fifty guineas.

Feeling well satisfied with themselves, Leonora and Jane next visited Beau Monde, where they whiled away two or three pleasant hours trying on various bonnets, toques, caps, and turbans.

Guiding Jane away from a purple creation trimmed with silk daisies, Leonora soon had her outfitted with several becoming bonnets, a little brown velvet toque to wear with her riding habit, and a carriage bonnet of a blue that exactly matched her eyes. For herself, Leonora chose a striped toque of marigold and orange watered satin, trimmed with straw feathers, a duchesse bonnet in bronze velvet with a corsage of canary silk ribbons, and a simple little blue cap that tilted most rakishly over one eye, and was trimmed with a sweeping white plume.

Next, they stopped at one of Vienna's charming little cafés, where they sat outside beneath a gay striped awning, sipping the thick, sweet coffee and losing a great deal of their self-control over the thick, creamy pastries as they watched the world go by them.

"You know, I think that is the czar over there," Jane whispered at one point to Leonora, pointing to a tall, fair gentleman in a military uniform, strolling along the boulevard taking the air.

"Oh, it couldn't be," Leonora replied, dabbing at her lips with a napkin and trying very hard not to stare. "Czars don't just go strolling about in public without a guard or an equerry or someone."

"I saw him in London last spring, with his odious sister, and I am certain that is he," Jane insisted.

"Pardon me, madam," their waiter said in stiff English, "but, yes, that is the czar. He strolls by here every day. This is Vienna. He knows that here no one will bother him." There was pride in the man's voice.

"My goodness," Jane said, and at that moment the gentleman turned, and seeing two attractive ladies, doffed his hat and bowed.

There was no mistaking the order pinned to his blue coat. He *was* the czar. Jane and Leonora bowed in return, and watched wide-eyed as he strolled along his way, just another person taking the September air.

"My, what a strange place!" Leonora said. "Could you imagine poor Prinny out on the strut? He would probably be pelted with rotten tomatoes. I know I have frequently felt as if I should like to!"

Jane sipped her coffee. "Evidently, the czar's sister did, in a manner of speaking. She was dreadfully rude to him when the Russians were in London. But I heard that she was dreadfully rude to everyone, except poor Princess Charlotte."

I suppose this is the sort of information they will wish me to collect, Leonora thought unhappily. And I know nothing of politics at all! Even Jane, who is a chit of a schoolgirl, knows more than I!

Leonora could console herself with the fact that she did know about clothes, for their next stop was the mantua maker, where Jane was outfitted from head to foot with new chemises, stays, petticoats, and stockings, and Lady Leonora purchased a chinoiserie-embroidered dressing gown, covered with dragons and demons. She declared putting it on in the morning would serve as her best defense against Strawbridge.

Their last visit was to the shoemaker, an elderly German man of such frailty that they were both certain he would keel over as he bent to take their measurements. But there must be satin dancing slippers, and many of them, for their soles were so thin they could be danced through in a single evening and then cast aside. Jane's only pair of shoes was in the most pitiful condition, for she had worn them all the way across Europe, and against her better judgment, Leonora purchased a pair of ready-made slippers of the sort that would fit either foot, however painfully, and were worn until they stretched to conform to the shape of the foot. Both of them ordered half-boots of orange jean, for they were indispensable for walking, and Jane was fitted for a pair of riding boots. Leonora broke down and ordered a pair of orange-and-white-striped satin slippers, declaring she was quite unable to resist their charm, even though she was not entirely certain they would go with anything she owned.

From there, it was the glovemaker, the perfumer, and again, helpless against temptation, a little café where they had glaces.

"If we keep this up," Jane mourned on the way home, "I shall not be able to fit into any of my clothes at all."

Before they had descended from the barouche, Chandler had opened the door to them and was dispatching a footman for their packages.

Leonora looked at Jane a trifle oddly, but Miss Hobart, who had grown up around her father's butler, appeared to notice nothing amiss.

"Good afternoon, ladies," Chandler greeted them gravely. "It would appear that while you were out, my lady, your majordomo has been quite busy."

"Oh, dear," Leonora said, envisioning a conflict between her servants and Sir Julian's, as she undid the strings of her bonnet and peeled off her gloves.

Jane had impulsively rushed on ahead, and thrust her head through the door of the Yellow Saloon. "Lady Leonora! Do come and look!" she exclaimed.

Expecting the worst, Leonora peered around Jane's head through the doorway. "Why, it's a completely different room!" she exclaimed.

Indeed it was. Gone from the walls were the hideous tapestries, which were replaced by some of the more tasteful family portraits. A great deal of the bric-a-brac had disappeared, leaving only a handful of the more attractive pieces situated about the room. The massive pieces of furniture had been rearranged into small, intimate groupings, and by some means the mildew was gone from the rug. The curtains had been parted and held back to allow the sunshine to flow into the room, and by some miracle possible only through René's genius, fresh flowers were everywhere.

"Oh, my," Leonora repeated.

"If you will pardon me for saying so, my lady, it does make quite a difference," Chandler said quietly. "One might almost believe one was in an English drawing room."

"Oh, come and look at what he's done with the Blue Room!" Jane called. "And the Green Salon, and the dining room . . ."

Indeed, the whole downstairs had been transformed. What had been darkly oppressive and gloomy before had become light, airy, and welcoming.

"Yes, I think one may now entertain here graciously," Lady Leonora murmured to herself. René, she decided, was worth every penny of his astronomical salary.

"I believe, my lady, that your majordomo is belowstairs conferring with the new chef," Chandler intoned.

"The new chef?"

He nodded in assent. "As you may have noticed, my lady, we have been forced to make do with a quite inferior person in the kitchen."

Thinking of last night's meal, which had

been overcooked, smothered in tasteless sauces, and arrived at the table cold, Leonora was forced to agree.

"It would seem that M. D'Aubusson encountered an old acquaintance on the street. A person he had known from better days, before the Revolution, who has now been reduced to the position of chef. If I may say so, my lady, it is to be hoped that Beaumain can cook. Sir Julian's digestion has been sadly dyspeptic since we arrived in Vienna. All those heavy state dinners, and then to come home to Gaffelplatz's cooking." Chandler shook his head.

"I do hope René has not tried to usurp your place, Chandler. He can be terribly managing," Leonora started apologetically.

"On the contrary, my lady. When I entered service with Sir Julian, it was to serve as his valet. Butling has never been my calling, really. It will be a relief to turn those chores over to a person who seems to enjoy them, and return to devoting myself to the care of Sir Julian's wardrobe."

Leonora nodded, quite uncertain of what to say.

"Miss Strawbridge, my lady, a most excellent person, if I may be permitted to say so, has had a day of rest and seems to be recovering nicely from her ordeal."

"That's good, for I shall need her to dress me for dinner tonight, I suppose. Has Sir Julian made any plans for this evening?"

"I believe that you will be dining at the legation. Lady Castlereagh is most anxious to see Miss Jane, and of course, make your acquaintance."

Leonora nodded again.

Chandler cleared his throat. "Pardon me, my lady, but do you dance the waltz?"

"The waltz?" Leonora repeated blankly.

Chandler nodded. "It is a new dance, and all the rage in Vienna. The gentleman places his hand upon the lady's waist, and procures her other hand at shoulder level. Then they glide about the floor."

"He puts his hand on her *waist*?"

Chandler nodded. "I only ask because I am sure that Lord Castlereagh will ask. He is trying desperately to learn, and will beg any lady who can waltz to be his partner."

"Thank you, Chandler," Lady Leonora said, and went up to her room, completely in a daze.

The British legation had rented quarters first in a tiny street with the odd name of Im Ange Gottes, but as the number of plenipotentiaries, diplomatists, aides, equerries, secretaries, and servants swelled, it became necessary to move to larger quarters, and a magnificent suite of twenty-two rooms on the Minoriztenplatz, a most charming square, was selected as the new home for the British legation.

It was, Lady Leonora decided as she entered a magnificently stately reception hall on the arm of Sir Julian, a wise choice. Close to the Hofburg, where the emperor hosted the czar and the King of Prussia, and a short walk from the Chancellery, where the all-powerful Prince Metternich held sway, it seemed the ideal setting to represent

English ways as exemplified by Lord and Lady Castlereagh.

As they received their guests, they were, Leonora thought, anything but imposing. Lord Castlereagh was tall, not particularly well favored, and spoke with the rough, somewhat abrupt tones of the very shy. And yet his smile was charming, and the warmth with which he greeted Jane was sincere, complimenting her on how well she had turned out since last he had seen her in pigtails. His greeting to Lady Leonora was equally friendly, and he seemed greatly pleased to recall that he had been at school with one of her cousins. Lady Castlereagh, fat, frumpy, and frequently eccentric in her dress, embraced Jane to her massive bosom, recalled her late mother with affection, and declared that she would be just as great a beauty as that unfortunate female.

"I begin to understand why your father says invitations to a casual dinner here are prized above those to an imperial state ball," Leonora remarked to Jane as she accepted a glass of champagne from a passing waiter. "The Castlereaghs might just as easily be Darby and Jane by the fireside of their own home."

"Dear Lady C. You know she held me in my cradle," Jane replied. "Yes, they are above all things comfortable people, anxious to make one feel at home."

"I look about the room," Sir Julian said, coming up beside them, "and I see many beautiful ladies, but none so fine as those I escort tonight."

Leonora and Jane both felt that they had reason to be pleased with themselves, for Strawbridge had outdone herself in turning them out as elegantly as she could. Leonora wore a gown of silver net over a slip of celestial-blue sarcenet, richly trimmed with turns of striped blue and silver satin at sleeve and décolletage, the wadded hem draped in pointe-de-Belgique lace caught with tiny white silk rosebuds. About her arms she had draped a silver spangled shawl of spiderweb gauze, and her gleaming curls were dressed *à la grecque*. She wore her diamond necklace and a pair of pearl-and-diamond teardrop earrings. Over one gloved elbow she had hung a silver lamé reticule.

Jane, as befitted a debutante, wore a gown of palest peach crepe, with a slashed sleeve revealing silk of a deeper peach. Her hem was caught by tiny silk scallops of the same deep peach, revealing a froth of Venice lace beneath. Tiny baroque pearls, a loan from Leonora's overflowing jewel case, hung from the lobes of her ears, and a single baroque pearl on a golden chain was clasped about her slender neck. Strawbridge had dressed her blond locks in a simple style, with a topknot and a few curls seeming to escape their bondage, falling most charmingly about her face. This was her first adult party, and her eyes flashed with excitement and a becoming flush flooded through her cheeks.

She looked, Leonora thought, utterly charming, and catching the look Sir Julian was giving his daughter, she realized that his thoughts must be similar to her own.

These new arrivals to the scene inevitably attracted a great deal of attention, and in very short order Sir Julian had made them known to Sir Charles Stewart, to whom Lady Leonora took an instant dislike that was to prove to be correctly founded, Lord Clencarty, Sir Edward Cooke, and Joseph Planta. Those, he announced, were the big guns of the delegation. There was also a host of young men somehow or other connected to the delegation who very soon were clustered about the laughing Jane, who seemed to need no lessons in the way in which to conduct a light flirtation.

"I see that we shall have no trouble at all finding suitors for Jane," Lady Leonora laughed.

"Ah, they may look like a pack of young bucks, but believe me, Cooke works them hard enough," Sir Julian replied. "Keeps them out of trouble, don't you know."

"At their age, they will work all day and dance all night and still find time for a ride in the park in the morning," Leonora sighed.

"Julian! You do not come last night, *et je suis dévastée!*" exclaimed a darkly beautiful woman in an extremely low-cut dress, walking up to Sir Julian and tapping him with her fan upon the arm, in a manner that Lady Leonora could only consider most flirtatious.

Sir Julian flushed. "Well, Princess, there were . . . er, circumstances which prevented me from making my . . . er, arrival. My daughter appeared suddenly on my doorstep, you see."

The dark woman pouted with rouged lips,

her ample bosom heaving with indignation, whether false or real, Leonora could not tell.

"I attend, and I attend, and I do not see you. Only a note in English, which I cannot read!"

"My apologies, Princess. It will not happen again, I assure you," Sir Julian said.

"I think not. I think that I shall, how do you say? Set up a flirt with the very handsome Lord Umberto. He will not leave me waiting!"

"Ah, Princess, please allow me to introduce you to Lady Leonora Ware, the English lady who accompanied my daughter to Vienna and will be acting as my hostess." Sir Julian smiled. "Lady Leonora, may I present the Princess Bagration? She is quite the most powerful female in Vienna. More powerful, perhaps, than even Metternich."

The princess's laughter pealed out. Her good humor quite restored, she took Lady Leonora's hand in her own. "How do you do? You are very pretty, although much in the English style. I too am pretty, but in the Russian way, which is entirely different!"

"Lady Leonora will be bringing my daughter out with a ball at our house," Sir Julian said.

The princess nodded. "Ah, I begin to see! *Vous êtes comme Talleyrand et la pauvre Dorothea Courland, non?*"

"*Mais non!*" Sir Julian said firmly. "The arrangement is entirely respectable, *je vous assure!*"

The princess's peal of laughter rang out again, and she tapped Sir Julian on the arm with her open fan. "*Les anglais,* always so respectable! It is very droll, you know! Or do I mean very dull? Whatever! Lady Leonora, you must come and ride in my carriage with me. It will make you very stylish, for I am very fashionable here. I think that I must find you a lover! Every woman in Vienna should have at least one lover."

Leonora was not certain whether to be shocked or amused, but she could not help but like this airy little Russian with the silver laugh.

"I should be delighted to ride with you, Princess," she said.

"Very good! It is settled, then. My carriage shall call for you at eleven tomorrow morning, if I am awake by then. Should you like to bring the ravishing Miss Hobart?"

"Absolutely not, Catherine!" Sir Julian said firmly.

She fluttered her long dark lashes at him. "I shall promise to be the very model of propriety in the style English," she promised demurely. "Besides, I should much enjoy the rage and jealousy that cat Sagan shall feel when she sees that I have captured the two lovely English ladies first!"

"The Duchess of Sagan and the Princess Bagration are neighbors," Sir Julian explained. "Each one has rented a wing of the Palm Palace for the duration of the Congress."

"And Wilhelmina and I thoroughly detest each other!" Princess Bagration said cheerfully. "She cannot bear my dear cousin the czar, and I have no liking for Prince Metternich, with whom she is *très intime.*" The princess sighed.

"So hard on poor Laure Metternich, with all those children." She opened her fan and flapped it at herself rapidly. "But there, I see my lord Umberto coming this way!"

In his usual black evening dress, Umberto seemed suave and elegant, even in this crowd, as he approached their group, a twisted smile on his dark face.

He bowed over the princess's hand. "Ah, madam, I hope I find you well?" he asked. "As usual, you are ravishing."

Her silver laugh pealed out. "Umberto, you are a heartless flirt," she cooed.

"Yes, I suppose that I am," he replied equably, surveying Leonora's gown with approval. "And I trust, my lady, that I find you well this evening?" he asked, taking up her hand in his own. "How do you find our humble abode?"

"Most interesting," Leonora admitted. "Everything is new and different. I fear that I shall have trouble learning to go on. But the princess has been kind enough to invite me to go out in her carriage tomorrow, so I think that I shall learn a great deal."

"Take care that you do not learn too much," he murmured into his hand.

"Do you speak from your own experience?" Leonora retorted from behind her fan.

"But there, I see dear Charles Stewart. How handsome he is," said the princess, her eyes hungry as a cat's. "I will go and talk to him, for he must know how the meeting at the Chancellery went today. . . ."

In a cloud of heavy scent, she drifted away.

Sir Julian heaved an audible sigh of relief. "Damned treacherous female. It is she and not Alexander who should have been czar."

"They say that she has his ear as no other woman save his sister does," Umberto muttered. "They also say that she is on his gold."

"Wonder where she finds the time, between her lovers. Insatiable female! Pardon me, Lady Leonora," Sir Julian added apologetically.

"Oh, I quite understand," Leonora said, sipping her champagne. "I am learning very fast, you see."

"That's the ticket!" Umberto exclaimed jovially. "Ride with her tomorrow, and see what you will learn."

"Doubtless I shall pick up nothing that she has not already taught you," Leonora murmured. Did she feel a stab of jealousy, or was it merely too much champagne?

"I say, old man," Sir Julian exclaimed. "Is that not old All-Things-to-All-Men I see greeting old Castlereagh?"

"By God, Julian, I do believe it is Talleyrand himself, the old devil. How came he to be in Vienna, and who invited him tonight?"

The unexpected entrance of the wily man who had been Bonaparte's foreign minister until the emperor's defeat, upon which event he had suddenly offered his services to the restored Bourbons, caused a ripple throughout the room. As the old statesman, bewigged and clubfooted and wearing the order of the Fleur de Lys upon his chest, greeted Lord and Lady Castlereagh, Umberto's shoulders shook with silent laughter.

"By God, you must hand it to him for being a complete hand! Mark my words, he has come to the Congress to make certain that there are not four powers, but five!"

"I should not be surprised," Sir Julian mused. "Was there ever a trickier devil!"

"Only one, and here he comes across the room, as smooth as silk, old Metternich himself!" Umberto exclaimed.

Fascinated, Leonora watched as the two most powerful men in Europe bowed in greeting to one another. Metternich, dark, tall, well-formed, and well-mannered, and the white-wigged, slightly stooped, fox-faced Talleyrand. All eyes were upon them as they exchanged a few words, and then, at some jest Talleyrand made, both men burst into laughter and turned away, easing off the tension.

Lady Castlereagh seized upon Prince Metternich's arm, and he escorted her toward the dining room as other couples followed suit.

The promise of food broke the tension as nothing else could, and the incident was soon forgotten as a homely veal ragout was placed before them.

It was plain that the Castlereaghs believed in simple English cooking, Leonora decided.

As she took her seat, she was surprised to see a vaguely familiar face placed to her right. Smiling uncertainly, she removed her napkin from its ring and tried to think of the gentleman's name, certain that she had encountered him before. Even his plain blue tunic seemed familiar to her, although she could not place it in her mind.

"So, we meet again," the gentleman said in heavily accented English.

"Yes, we meet again," Leonora agreed pleasantly. "But unfortunately, sir, I am unable to recall your name."

The gentleman chuckled as a footman ladled soup into his plate. "Alexander," he said.

Leonora looked puzzled. "Alexander? I am afraid you have the better of me, sir."

"Perhaps you would recall Czar Alexander?" he asked gently.

"Oh, my," was all that Leonora could think of to say. "Of course! On the Undenplatz. You were walking by and Jane and I were eating glaces!"

"Precisely! It would be hard to forget two such lovely ladies as yourselves. And you are?"

"Lady Leonora Ware, sir."

He nodded affably. "Ah, yes, the English lady who will serve as Sir Julian Hobart's hostess. Yes. A most excellent choice. I hope that you will do me the honor to invite me to Sir Julian's parties. Do you dance?"

"Yes, but not the waltz. I have not yet learned it," she admitted.

The czar shook his head. "Ah, but you must learn it at once, madam! Not to dance the waltz is to be as nothing in Vienna!"

"So I am given to understand, sir. I shall have to engage a dancing instructor for myself and my charge at once."

The czar shook his head and winked. "No,

no, is not necessary! After the dinner, Lord Castlereagh's musicians will play, and we shall ask them to play the waltz, and I shall teach you. I waltz very well, you see!"

"Oh, sir, I couldn't possibly—" Leonora protested.

"Castlereagh will waltz. Lady Castlereagh will waltz also. So will Sir Charles Stewart, and the Prince of Württemberg. So, you will waltz with me!"

"Oh, my," Lady Leonora said, charmed in spite of herself.

The czar smiled. "Do not forget," he commanded her as the courses changed and he turned to the lady on his left.

The gentleman to Lady Leonora's right was both breathtakingly handsome and covered with decorations. He introduced himself as Prince Adam Czartroyski, and gazed at her with such large and soulful brown eyes that she felt as if her heart were quite ready to melt. He was much in the Byronic mode, and full of passionate speeches about the freedom of Poland, to which she listened politely, having little idea what he wished to free Poland from. But it seemed to her to be a very good idea that Poland should be free, and she hoped its liberation would be one of the outcomes of the Congress, if only for the sake of this handsome young gentleman. Perhaps the wines were going to her head, perhaps she was merely naive. But she suddenly realized that she had a great deal to learn about what was going on in Vienna.

Glancing across the table, she saw Jane

talking in earnest and animated tones to a tall, rather melancholy gentleman who seemed only to pick at his food as he listened, his heavy visage lightened from time to time by a smile.

"I wonder what the young lady says who can hold the interest of the King of Denmark?" the prince asked curiously. "She is very lovely, and I have not seen her before."

Jane, Leonora realized, having spent a lifetime in political and diplomatic circles, was able to discourse easily and without restraint to a king, while she struggled to understand why Poland must be liberated. "That, Prince, is Miss Jane Hobart, Sir Julian's daughter. She is barely out, but as Sir Julian's hostess, I will be presenting her at a ball very shortly."

The prince smiled. "I should very much like to meet her," he breathed.

Leonora rather doubted that Sir Julian would wish his daughter to become involved with anyone so radical as this handsome Polish prince, so she smiled and promised nothing.

Down the board, Umberto was drinking red wine and smiling his crooked smile upon quite the most beautiful female Leonora had ever seen. The lady was fair, with a complexion so clear and delicate that she might have been made of porcelain, and when she smiled, she exposed a row of perfect white teeth.

"Who is that, if you please?" Leonora asked the prince.

"That, Lady Leonora, is the Countess Julie Zichy. You have no doubt heard of her. No? Amazing! She breaks all hearts, not only with her beauty, but because she is a true and faithful wife to her count, so much in love with him that she looks at no other man, not even the czar."

"She seems to be one of the few virtuous females here, then," Leonora remarked. "Save for Emily Castlereagh."

"Things are very much different in Europe, my lady, than in your England," the prince replied. "Romance and politics entwine in Vienna."

"So I see," Leonora murmured, making a note to herself that she must sit down and have a very long talk with Jane.

After the board had been cleared and the covers removed, Lady Castlereagh led the ladies away to a small rose salon. Large and motherly, she placed herself upon a settee, all her bracelets jangling on her thick arms as she poured out tea and coffee, chattering amiably to anyone who might come within her reach. With her dark hair piled up beneath a quite amazing purple turban trimmed with ostrich feathers and a gray silk dress pinned all over with an assortment of brooches, she was a quiz, but her sharp dark eyes, set beneath heavy brows, missed nothing, and Leonora had the sudden feeling, as she accepted a tiny demitasse laden with whipped cream and sugar in the Viennese manner, that Castlereagh pillow talk must be quite interesting.

Princess Bagration accepted a glass of sherry from a passing footman and seated herself in a flurry of shawls at the carved rosewood pianoforte, idly picking out a few melancholy Russian tunes. It seemed clear to Leonora that this highly political female obviously bored with the company of women, yearned to be back in the dining room, smoking cigars and drinking port and brandy with the men, participating in the talk about the future of Europe. The princess glanced up, and as if she had read Leonora's thoughts, gave a most unaristocratic wink.

When all the ladies had been served, and were drifting about the drawing room, their trains rustling on the floors, their voices murmuring in genteel tones, Lady Castlereagh heaved herself to her feet with a grunt, patted about herself for all her brooches, and took Jane and Leonora about the room to introduce them to the others.

"The ladies are the ones who really wield the power in Vienna," Lady Castlereagh said only half in jest. "It is important that you know them."

Jane and Leonora were introduced first to the Duchess of Sagan, a tall, thin sandy-haired woman with a long nose and eyes so pale and clear that they seemed to look right through everyone. This was the lady who shared the Palm Palace with Princess Bagration, and no one could have been more that lady's opposite. Where the princess was unrestrained and forthcoming, the duchess was cool and reserved. Even the neck of her pale blue silk dinner dress was high and trimmed with lace, while her only ornament was a rope of magnificently matched pearls. It seemed to Leonora that there was a trace of melancholy about her, as if she had experienced a great deal of sadness in her life. But she exclaimed a great deal over Jane's fair beauty and promised that she would leave cards upon them, if they would but come to one of her evenings. "They are not at all grand or formal, you see, but everyone comes to *my* side of the palace."

The princess at the pianoforte made a face at her rival's back.

"I am sure that Metternich would very much like to see you both there," she added. "Lovely women please him so much."

"Thank you," Leonora murmured, a little stunned that the duchess should thus mention so casually her relationship with Prince Metternich, a married man who had four children.

Leonora had no way of knowing that the duchess had borne, and been forced to give away, a natural child who would have been close to Jane's age.

They were introduced to a string of minor German princesses, dull and chubby little things with bad English and guttural French, who seemed more interested in the coffee pastries than the two English ladies, chattering away among themselves in their own language.

"Countess Julie Zichy," Lady Castlereagh puffed, a little out of breath, "may I present Lady Leonora Ware and Miss Jane Hobart, Sir Julian's daughter."

The beautiful little countess, barely out of the schoolroom and married not quite a year to her diplomat husband, held out her tiny hand with a breathtaking smile. "How do you do?" she asked shyly, dropping her long lashes against her cheeks. "It is so very charming to meet you,

Lady Leonora, Miss Hobart. I see Miss Hobart at the dining table and I think: oh, a *jeune fille comme moi!* Perhaps she will be *gentille et douce* and we will be able to have conversations!"

"I think that would be above all things famous," Jane replied sincerely. "I know how very hard it can be when you are so much younger than everyone else, and no one quite understands what to do with you!"

"Exactly so. They all want to set up the flirtation, or the women, they do not like me. *C'est triste.*" She twisted her fan in her hands and turned her ravishing face up toward Jane, who linked her arm into the other girl's.

"Come, we shall take a turn about the room and talk, if you like!"

Lady Castlereagh chuckled. "Well! It is a good thing to see two rival beauties form an alliance! I have never seen a gel more head over heels with her husband than Julie Zichy, and yet all the men have been trying to set up flirts with her! It is a great deal too bad, for she's a nice little soul and doesn't know how to repulse 'em!" Lady Castlereagh toyed with a brooch on her bosom, and clasped Leonora's arm. "There's Sagan's little sister, Dorothea, Countess Talleyrand Périgord. Talleyrand brought her along to Vienna to serve as his hostess, but I daresay you may imagine what their relationship might be. She's married to his nephew, you know. Of course, my dear, it was a dreadful *mésalliance* from the start, but Talleyrand and the poor chit's mother were having an affair, so there you have it, they arranged it between the pair of

them. Talleyrand! That dreadful, oily man. He
reminds me of nothing so much as one of our
tinkers in Ireland, conniving and contriving!
Well, you must of course meet *her*. She has
prettiness and charm, and amazingly enough,
she's quite well-educated!"

Like a fighting ship with a bark in tow, Lady
Castlereagh bore down upon Countess Périgord
with Lady Leonora in hand.

As the ambassadress made the introduction,
Leonora took the other woman in. She was as
dark as her sister was fair, thinly made, with
brown eyes so enormous that they seemed to
take over her heart-shaped face, framed becomingly in dark and lustrous curls.

Leonora found her to be perfectly charming
and gay, with a sharp wit and a very shrewd
intelligence that she seemed at some pains to
conceal.

They found a mutual topic in the subject of
the arduous journey from Paris to Vienna, and
the many hardships they had endured along the
way. Both ladies being used to their comforts,
they were easily able to commiserate upon their
discomforts, and Countess Périgord was suitably
horrified at the tale of Lady Leonora's adventure
in Linz.

"Talleyrand had outriders, of course." Dorothea shuddered. "Or heaven only knows that
the same fate would have befallen us!"

From there, the subject shifted to that of
entertaining in a strange house and a foreign
land. "Of course, a good majordomo is indispensable, and a good chef one of the blessings

of life, but still, one has to think of everything oneself, so that it may be just so," Dorothea mused. "Perhaps if Talleyrand does not object, I may be able to lend our good Careme for your ball."

"That would be wonderful!" Leonora enthused. "Should you ever need the services of my René, you only need ask," she added. "He is a miracle worker at all things!"

"I seem to find you ladies gossiping like a pair of good hausfraus," said an amused voice, and they both turned to see Talleyrand standing beside them, a sardonic smile on his face as he surveyed Leonora from head to toe.

Something about him made her uneasy, and she felt a flush creeping into her cheeks. But Dorothea gazed up at her lover adoringly. "Lady Leonora and I have been discussing entertaining in Vienna. She gives a ball for her—niece?— Miss Hobart, Sir Julian's daughter. Oh! I am forgetting that you have met. Prince Talleyrand, you recall my lady Leonora Ware, who is Sir Julian Ware's hostess!"

Talleyrand took Leonora's hand in his own and bowed over it stiffly, his shrewd eyes never leaving her face, his smile betraying his enjoyment of her uneasiness.

"Ah, yes, Lady Leonora! I have heard of your adventures on the road! Most distressing for you, I am sure!"

"I fear my lord Umberto has been dining out upon the tale! It was nothing, really." She forced herself to keep her voice light.

"Ah, I did not hear it from Umberto." His

smile was thin. "I have other sources, my lady."

I would imagine that you do, Leonora thought, but refused to give him the satisfaction of telling her his sources were a dark secret.

"Is that Sir Julian's daughter strolling arm in arm with La Zichy? What a pretty picture they do make. I understand you plan a ball for Miss Hobart?"

"Yes. She is not really out yet, you know."

"Ah, but in Vienna, every young miss is already out." He laughed. "I hope, Dorothea, that you have invited Lady Leonora to bring Miss Hobart to call? Our direction is of course the Kaunitz Palace."

"Of course," Leonora said politely. "And I sincerely hope that you will call upon us, Countess, at the Friezenhaus."

"It will be my pleasure, Lady Leonora," Dorothea assured her warmly.

"Signatory!" Lady Leonora muttered to herself, opening her fan. She was uncertain what the word meant, save it expressed her feelings. Females, she knew, were more valuable allies to another female than any man. If she were to launch Jane successfully, she would need the support of every one of the important ladies she had met tonight.

It would seem, she thought, fanning herself furiously, that this thing of being political was as complex and subtle as the art of being tonishly fashionable. Well, Leonora had been tonish for several years without putting a great deal of effort into it, so she began to think that perhaps she might learn to be political without a great deal of trouble.

Even as she had been talking to Talleyrand, the gentlemen, led by Lord Castlereagh, had left the port to join the ladies, and the salon was filling with somber black evening dress and brightly colored uniforms trimmed in gold braid, mingling among the sumptuous evening dresses and the sparkling jewels.

Footmen were opening the doors between the drawing room and the adjoining salon, and Leonora saw that musicians had set up their stands, ready to play the first yearning strains of the waltz.

"Ah!" exclaimed Castlereagh with great pleasure, seizing up his dowdy little wife in his arms and whirling her about the floor. It was easy to tell by the way that they smiled at each other that they were still deeply in love, and even the coldest heart must have been touched by such a scene.

Out of the corner of her eye, Leonora saw Umberto leading Princess Bagration to the floor, taking her lightly in his arms, and swirling her about, her shawls flying.

"Lady Leonora? You have promised me!"

She turned to see the czar smiling eagerly at her. "I am honored, sir," she said. "But you must recall, I am a novice!"

"Ah, my lady, it is so simple. I place my hand upon your waist, you place yours upon mine. *Eh bien!* Now, you must give me your other hand, held like so, yes! And now, take a moment to listen to the rhythm of the music, and then,

I glide about the floor with you, round and round and round!"

"Sir, I believe that I am waltzing!" Leonora exclaimed a little giddily. "Oh, it is wonderful!"

"You do very well, Lady Leonora." The czar smiled. "And now, we turn, and turn again, like so! There! You dance the waltz!"

"I do believe that I am! With the Czar of Russia, of all persons!"

"Ah, my lady, forget that I am a czar, and think only of me as a man who has admired you deeply since first I saw you."

It was nothing more than a light flirtation, and Leonora responded in like manner. How funny it was that the czar should be like any other man, only perhaps more whimsical, she thought, much amused. Indeed, had she planned on grandchildren, which she did not, this would have been something to tell them. How much more interesting to be here than in London at some sad squeeze at Lady Jersey's, or a very dull play. This was a time and place that would never happen again, and she was glad that she was playing a part, however minor, in it.

9

"D'YOU THINK PAPA has had an *affaire* with her?" Jane asked, peering out the curtains of the Yellow Saloon in search of Princess Bagration's barouche coming up the street.

"Jane! What a terrible question to ask!" Leonora said disapprovingly, running a gloved finger down René's lists of persons to be invited to Jane's ball.

"Well, Papa does have *affaires*, you know. I've known forever and ever about it. I keep hoping he will marry one of them and settle down with her, but he never does. Do you think he will marry the Princess Bagration? Then at least she wouldn't have that awful name. Bag Ration. It sounds like something you would pack in your kit for a march through Spain."

Leonora's lips twitched beneath her yellow chamois carriage bonnet, and it was hard to make her voice severe as she said, "You are not to discuss such matters with the princess or anyone else. Jane, perhaps you and I should have a talk about . . . certain matters between men and women."

Miss Hobart toyed with the buttons on her pelisse. "If you mean what I think you mean, Lady Leonora, I've known all about that forever. Well, for a good while, anyway. One of the maids at school told us all about it."

"I can just imagine," Leonora said dryly.

"I thought it sounded dreadful, but Julie Zichy says when you are in love it is better than anything in the whole world. She and Felix—"

"Never mind about the Count and Countess Zichy," Leonora said quickly.

"But Princess Bagration, I don't understand. She is said to be very *fast*, and yet she goes everywhere and does everything, and no one shuns her."

"I suppose things are different in Europe," Leonora said, tapping a pencil against her teeth. Did one really want Felix Schwarzenberg at Jane's come-out? "She, unlike you or I, is a princess of royal Russian blood, a divorcée, has a great deal of money, and can do exactly as she pleases. What she pleases to do and with whom is none of our business. She is a very powerful woman who can be of great help to your father, an important hostess who can help to make your come-out and your season here a great success, and last, she is a very charming female with a great deal of style and panache."

"She is also twenty minutes late," Jane said, glancing at the clock.

"Yes, I suppose she is. When we went home last night, dead on our feet, she was still dancing."

"Leonora, did you happen to meet a Prince Adam Czartroyski?" Jane asked innocently, threading the curtain fringe through her fingers.

"I was seated beside him at dinner," Leonora said carefully.

"Is he not the most romantic, the most handsome, the most gallant man you have ever seen?" Jane continued dreamily.

"He is certainly enough to take one's breath away, but a dead bore upon the subject of Poland. It was all that he could talk about."

"But Poland is very important!"

"Yes, I agree with you. The fate of Poland is important. But certainly not as a constant subject for discussion at the dinner table."

It was fortunate that Chandler chose that moment to inform the ladies that Princess Bagration's barouche was waiting outside, and the subject was dropped.

Catherine Bagration greeted them lazily, draped gracefully into a corner of her peach-satin-lined barouche, propped up by a number of cushions, and carrying a lacy parasol against the pale sunlight. Her dark curls were covered by a very dashing hat of Circe-green panne velvet, with several yarrow-yellow plumes sweeping down to brush her cheek. Even the neck of her carriage dress was cut quite low to expose her impressive bosom, and the thinnest gauze scarf had been draped across her throat, as if to protect some part of her thorax from the elements. The hem of her robe was deeply trimmed in lace, and upon her feet she wore pink-and-white-striped slippers.

"I bid you good morning," she drawled as Leonora and Jane were assisted into the carriage by a footman in the same peach livery. "I suppose I am late, but I am always late, you know. I have no sense of time."

As soon as the ladies were settled, she signaled the coachman on, and the team, four lively matched grays, set to a fine trot.

"Truly, I have scored a coup!" the princess laughed. "To be the first to be seen with the two lovely English ladies in my carriage will put Sagan's nose out of joint!"

Having lived in the city for a number of years, the princess was able to point out all the most interesting cathedrals, palaces, and sights with a wave of her parasol as they made their way to the park for the fashionable promenade. Here, beneath the lovely chestnut trees, slowly turning orange and gold in the autumn weather, it would seem that everyone in Vienna was to be seen taking the air in their very best attire. A festive spirit seemed to prevail, it seemed to Leonora, as it always did in Vienna, and she settled back against the peach-colored squabs to enjoy seeing and being seen. It was almost like a fairy tale, so many kings and princes, queens and duchesses, and all the European nobility gathered together in one place acting every bit as if they were no more than plain Herr Someone of Somewhere, or Frau This from This-and-that.

Having encountered her own sovereign only

once, and like many Englishmen, having no great liking for the erratic Prinny with his extravagant tastes and encroaching manners with pretty females, she found it somehow amusing to see so many more respectable members of royalty riding horseback like any other men, or simply strolling about unescorted by guards and equerries, chatting amiably with any person who might happen to cross their path. What a great release it must be for all of them to escape from the ceremonies and dignities of their offices and become, if only for a while, normal people, free of pretension and tradition, rubbing shoulders with the genial middle class merchants' wives and daughters of Vienna.

The czar, dressed very plainly in a dark tunic without decoration, and mounted on quite the most handsome Arabian Leonora had ever seen, rode up beside the princess's carriage and leaned down to give her a cousinly, Leonora hoped, kiss upon the cheek. "Good day, ladies! It adds a great deal of beauty to the landscape to see three such lovely females gathered together!" he exclaimed jovially, sweeping off his hat.

"Oh, sire, what a great go of a horse you have!" Jane exclaimed. "A capital piece of blood and bone!"

"Thank you, little one. He was a gift from Bonaparte, but we do not talk of that now, hey?" He winked and smiled. "And you, Lady Leonora, you do not forget how to do the waltz?"

"Not yet!" she replied. "But I fear that I shall need more practice!"

The czar laughed. "Believe me, you will have much practice indeed! There is a ball every night here, no, my dear Catherine?"

"Every single night," the princess agreed. "And all one does is waltz, waltz, waltz!"

"I go to the Chancellery now. Metternich and Talleyrand are already at loggerheads, but tonight perhaps I see you, Catherine?"

"Perhaps," she agreed, twirling her parasol.

With a courtly bow, the czar rode away. "My cousin will yet make trouble," the princess murmured to herself. "Poor Metternich!"

"What a cozy company," drawled a familiar voice, and Leonora looked up to see Umberto mounted upon a very dashing bay, grinning down at her most diabolically. "Good day, Princess, Miss Hobart! I see I find you in fashionable company!"

"There is no scandal in riding in the park," the princess said lazily. "But to my house, no, I cannot invite Miss Hobart!"

"See that you do not," Umberto said in a low voice.

"Why n—" Jane started to ask, and Leonora pressed the toe of her slipper against the girl's ankle.

"After that dreadful scandal with that poor Viennese miss and the Russian hussar? I am not like you, Umberto! I do not make the same mistake twice!" the princess exclaimed, frowning slightly. "Besides, it was not my fault. Her parents were there to look after her." She shook an admonishing finger at Jane. "Little one, do not go away into little rooms with hussars. It can only lead to trouble."

"No, I think I should probably not, if you say so," Jane replied doubtfully. "Although I cannot imagine why I would want to."

"Wait until you meet one!" Umberto laughed. "Dashing sorts of fellows!"

Leonora, feeling the conversation was taking a most improper turn, asked how things went at the Chancellery.

"Ah, Talleyrand's giving them proper what-for! It would appear that the four powers shall soon be five, if he has his say about it!"

"That fox!" Bagration laughed. "I am sure that his imperial highness will set him to rights soon enough, though!"

"I understand that Lady Leonora had a most interesting conversation with him last night," Umberto said, watching her intently.

Leonora shook her head. "And no desire to repeat the experience, either. He is an awful intriguer!"

"Ah, that is how he lands upon his feet again and again!" the princess laughed. "Well, Lord Umberto, did I expect to see you last night?"

Leonora twisted her fingers in her lap.

Umberto reined in his mount, and the horse danced excitedly. "I cannot say to that, my dear Princess. Perhaps we had our signals crossed."

"Perhaps. I entertain a few gentlemen for a little supper this evening. Perhaps you would care to be there, Umberto?" There was a faint hint of determination in her voice, and her eyes were dead serious.

Umberto shrugged lightly. "Who can tell? My ambassador may have need of me, and when duty calls, pleasure must wait."

The princess pouted very prettily.

"Although I should certainly hate to disappoint so lovely a lady," Umberto added, lifting the princess's hand to his lips.

The princess was suddenly all smiles again.

Jane was quite agog at this interchange, and Leonora could almost see her mind piecing it all together.

Umberto grinned at Leonora in quite the most annoying manner. Making his farewells, he rode away, and she felt very strongly that if she had had something to hand heavier than her reticule, she should have flung it at his head.

But the princess was all smiles as she bade her driver go on. "Your Englishmen have a certain charm all their own," she sighed. "Perhaps I shall marry one next."

She dropped them off at Sir Julian's at one, with the promise that Lady Leonora and Sir Julian should receive cards for her ball upon the twenty-first. She pronounced herself very well pleased with her new English friends, and promised to exert any influence she could in bringing Jane into society. Leonora, in spite of everything, found herself liking the princess very well, and they parted on good terms, promising to meet again at a very near date.

"But what I do not understand," Jane said to Leonora as they entered the house, "is why I should not be allowed to go to Princess Bagration's."

Leonora was casting about for a suitable way of explaining, when René appeared in the hallway, resplendent in a coat of bottle-green superfine. "Excuse me, madame, but Sir Julian has sent a messenger to announce that there will be twenty to dinner tonight. I thought you might like to cast an eye over the menu."

Relieved, Leonora allowed him to divest her of her coat and bonnet as she perused the menu. "It would seem all in order to me, René. As usual, you have outdone yourself."

He drew himself up to his full height. "Madame, it is a pleasure to entertain once again!" he said proudly. "To rise to the challenge of a great meal, to select the wines, to arrange the seating so that Prince Battenberg is not placed beside Madame Esterhazy—these are the things that are the meat and drink of my existence!"

"I am certain that they are," Leonora murmured. Clearly she need have no need to worry about René. He was in alt. She had not entertained lavishly since the death of her husband.

"I have also taken the liberty of setting the date for Miss Jane's ball for the seventeenth. It would seem that nothing else of importance will occur that evening, so we may be assured that everyone one would wish to have in attendance shall be present. I thought perhaps a supper for thirty-five couples, the receiving to start at nine, dancing at nine-fifteen, opening with a polonaise, refreshments at eleven, and champagne throughout would be appropriate. I have taken the liberty of engaging the decorator Moreau to do up the ballroom, madame, as he is certainly the most fashionable at the moment. The orchestra will of course be the Imperial Viennese, a little hard to engage, but they came around in the end with only a bit of persuasion and some of Sir Julian's English pounds. The *cartes d'invitation* have gone to the engravers, and I have taken the liberty of informing the Viennese police that there will be an entertainment that evening, so that traffic will not be impeded in the streets. Although," he added with a wink, "I am certain that they already knew, since it would seem to be their custom to keep a dossier on everyone and everything. It is my understanding the emperor finds it amusing bedtime reading."

Jane clapped her hands. "Oh, it sounds like bliss!" she exclaimed. "I am to come out at last!"

"And none too soon," Leonora added dryly.

"Incidentally, madame," René said, looking up at the gilt archways. "You and Miss Jane have appointments to have your likenesses made by the painter Isabey. It is all the rage to do so."

"Certainly Jane should have her likeness taken during her come-out, but there is no reason why I should sit—"

"Sir Julian's orders, my lady."

"Certainly it is very kind of him, but there is nothing I dislike more than sitting for hours and hours. When I sat for Lawrence . . ." She shrugged. "Well, no matter! I shall have to take it up with Sir Julian. Doubtless he thinks it a gift that would please me, but no, I think not."

"I shall wear pink, cut very low, and look heavenward, with a nosegay clutched to my breast," Jane announced, carried away by this vision of herself.

"For your sake, my dear, I certainly hope not. You will end up looking like a great booby, and in twenty years you will hide it away in the attic, only to have it discovered by your grand-children!" Leonora laughed, tweaking one of Jane's curls. "Believe me, I know! You should see the kit-kat done of me when I was your age! I cringe when I think of it! Now, I think that we would like some luncheon, and then you should have an hour's practice at the pianoforte before we put on our most comfortable shoes and trudge about the Hofburg admiring all the paint-ings we are supposed to admire."

"How like a governess you are becoming," Jane sighed. "Or a mother!" she added with a laugh.

René smirked behind his hand.

Sir Julian's dinner for twenty of the dullest guests Leonora had ever entertained seemed, in spite of her best efforts to be charming and interested, to drag on forever. There could be, she thought, nothing duller than a pack of minor aristocrats who held some claims to the attention of the British legation. The gentleman seated to her left had reminded her of nothing so much as the Duke of Clarence, fat, balding, and fiftyish, with a heavy accent and a decided tendency to place a thick hand on her knee beneath the covers until she had rapped his fingers sharply with the edge of her fan, all the while smiling her most charming smile. To her right had been

placed a Coburg prince whose obliviousness to
her existence had been surpassed only by the
way in which he had literally batted his eyelashes
at an uninterested René. She feared Sir Julian
did little better with a red-faced baroness squeezed
into a low-cut gown and a thin and haughty lady
wearing enough diamonds to qualify her as a
chandelier. Indeed, she rather envied Jane, dining *en famille* with Count and Countess Zichy
and several other young people.

Nonetheless, she did her best to be gracious,
even when, to her dismay, René's chef's carefully
prepared meal was wolfed down in fifteen minutes flat.

To withdraw the ladies from the table was
a positive ordeal, and she gave Sir Julian such a
woeful look that he was forced to smile behind
his napkin.

When the last guest had taken his leave, she
was able to throw herself gratefully into a chair,
kicking off her slippers and closing her eyes,
gratefully accepting the glass of sherry Sir Julian
offered and downing it in one gulp.

"Sorry about that, you know. But they are
important allies to us, and they must be entertained."

"Perhaps we should have sent them all to
Talleyrand's and let him entertain them," she
sighed, shaking her head. "Oh, I felt like nothing
so much as a pig-herder. Did you see the way
Baroness Zum Und Fliesch *gobbled* down the
ragout? I prayed devoutly not to laugh! René
shall give me his notice, I know!"

Sir Julian leaned against the mantel, smiling

down at her from beneath his blond brows. "You were magnificent, Lady Leonora! You were everything a diplomatic hostess should be! Gracious, charming, at ease, entertaining. They were impressed. And so was I."

Leonora opened her eyes. "Thank you, but it was nothing really but an ordeal."

"An ordeal you handled with expertise, ma'am! May I say that I am quite glad that you decided to stay with us. It has made a great deal of difference to both Jane and me."

"I am vastly enjoying myself, Sir Julian! It is most diverting for me, you know. I have never been a duenna, a spy, a hostess of the international set, nor . . . well, a great many things!"

"And yet you handle them all admirably, ma'am, if you will permit me to say so. I owe you a debt that I can never repay!"

"You owe me nothing, I assure you. I have never been so diverted in my life. It is all vastly amusing!"

"Indeed, Lady Leonora, I am glad that you are enjoying yourself. It means a great deal to me."

She looked at him from beneath her lashes, but said nothing.

"I had hoped that you would allow me to have your portrait taken by Isabey. I understand that he is all the fashion among the ladies," Sir Julian said slowly.

"And I had meant to speak to you about that. It is very kind of you, but I really do not want to sit for another painter. I have a very fine Lawrence at home and—"

"You mistake me, ma'am," Sir Julian said. "I had intended the portrait for myself."

She looked up at him, her brows rising slightly. When she saw that he was serious, she turned her head away, uncertain. The thought of Umberto, by now no doubt in the lovely arms of Princess Bagration, flickered through her mind. Did she feel a stab of jealousy at the thought? And Sir Julian was a handsome man, there was no doubt of that. She had thought so from the first moment she had seen him. And she loved Jane, as if she were her own daughter. . . .

"Well, aged ones, I have arrived home, upon the stroke of midnight, just as I said I would! Julie sent me off in her carriage!"

Jane entered the room, flushed and excited with her own evening, oblivious of the scene she had interrupted.

"Did you enjoy yourself, daughter?" Sir Julian asked as Lady Leonora rose and walked the length of the room, collecting her thoughts together, trying to will the flush away from her cheeks.

"Oh, famously! I have met ever so many wonderful gentlemen! I have promised them all that they may have a dance with me at my come-out, but I don't think there will be room on my dance card for all of them!" She giggled. "And what have you two been doing? Was it a terribly dull evening?"

"Oh, very dead indeed," Sir Julian said calmly. "But we shall hope for better in future, shall we not, Lady Leonora?"

"Yes, we shall hope for better in future," she repeated tonelessly.

Truly, Vienna was full of a sort of madness, but what to make of it when the last strains of the last waltz had been played?

10

AS THE COMINGS and goings of all inhabitants
and visitors to both the right and the left sides
of the Palm Palace were duly noted by the secret
police, and indeed, everyone else in Vienna, it
was generally known that Lord Umberto of the
British legation was regularly traveling up the
left set of stairs to the residence of Princess
Bagration at odd hours of the day and night.
Thus, he was acknowledged to be her latest lover
in a very long string, and such information was
accepted by everyone, including Lady Leonora
Ware.

   As for my lady, she was known to have paid
morning calls upon both Princess Bagration and
the Duchess of Sagan, and these ladies were
known to have paid morning calls upon her in
return.

   The secret police were having a great deal
more trouble determining what the relationship

might be between Lady Leonora Ware and Sir Julian Hobart. The footman in their employ could discover no evidence either way, and both Lady Leonora's and Sir Julian's servants were indignantly closed to bribery.

It might have been supposed, with the future of Europe being worked over and over daily at the Chancellery, that the secret police would have better and more interesting things to investigate, but this was, after all, Vienna, a city that thrived on gossip and intrigue and affairs of the heart, and for some reason, Emperor Franz had taken to following the course of events between these English as if it were a serial in a pulp magazine.

Perhaps it diverted him from the depressing thought that the Congress, which was supposed to have lasted eight weeks, had begun to look as if it would drag on forever, draining the state treasury further and further. Perhaps it was that his Hofburg Palace, while large and generally comfortable enough, was housing an increasingly expensive, demanding, and hard-to-please assortment of his royal relations from across Europe, all of them, from his cousin the czar down to the most minor Italian duke, quite touchy on matters of protocol. That they seemed to him to have arrived en masse on his doorstep with all their families, mistresses, staffs, servants, animals, and assorted hangers-on and showed not the slightest inclination to budge must have become depressing for him. They were beginning, as extended visitors will, to drive him and his frail and charming empress to distraction. State din-

ners can be amusing upon occasion, but to sit
down every night to one can become quite a
deterrent to good digestion.

Perhaps that was why his majesty decided
to ask Lord Castlereagh if it might be possible
to obtain a card for the ball for Miss Jane Hobart.
Doubtless he hoped that it would be a relief for
himself and his poor Maria Louisa. Or perhaps
he simply wanted to see this cast of English in
the flesh.

But when Leonora discovered that their
majesties would be graciously pleased to attend
the ball, she knew she had made a success.

In the week that preceded the ball, Sir Julian
Hobart found himself spending more and more
time at the legation, for it seemed to him that
there was no peace at all to be found in his own
home.

Wherever he settled himself with the news-
papers from England or a stack of dispatch cases,
there seemed to be a workman engaged upon
some mysterious activity involving paint, or car-
pets, or heaven only knew what mysteries of his
trade.

He barely laid eyes upon Lady Leonora,
who always seemed to be dashing to and fro, a
matronly lawn cap over her hair, a list of this or
that in her hand that must be taken care of
instantly. If, perchance, he found her standing
still in one place, she was in deep conference
with René or Chandler, and his sudden appearance somehow felt like an intrusion into some
deep and mysterious ritual to which fathers were
not party, although he could not of course help

but notice the mounting stack of tradesmen's bills on his secretary's desk.

Of his daughter, there seemed to be no trace whatsoever, although he might spot a cast-off bonnet on a hallway chair, or the edge of a skirt rustling around the corner of a stairs.

A bewildering number of nosegays of all manner of flowers had begun to pile up in the hallway, attached with notes in several languages and a great variety of masculine hands.

One day a haughty and fashionable lady passed him on the stairs, and he automatically bowed, only to discover later that the female was merely Madame Celeste, the modiste creating Jane's coming-out gown, leaving after a fitting.

Truly, it was all very disturbing, and he did not like having his house at sixes and sevens. Long widowed, he had long been used to living his life on his own way, and he began to suspect that, as the day of the event approached, nothing would be done by the time the guests arrived.

Nonetheless, that evening he descended from his carriage to step upon a red carpet leading up the flower-bedecked stairs, where two carved stone lanterns blazed forth into the night. He was greeted at the door by Chandler, who unceremoniously hustled his master up the stairs to his own quarters, where he was shaved, bathed, and fitted with the utmost care into his most elegant and formal evening attire, the old valet's trembling fingers working his cravat into the *trône d'amour* before having all of his decorations ceremoniously pinned to his chest.

"Damn, Chandler, it's only Miss Jane's presentation. I'm not handing up my credentials at court, you know," Sir Julian grumbled as the valet stepped back to admire his handiwork.

Nonetheless, when he descended the stairs to the landing, and heard a breathless voice above his head say, "Papa!" he turned to look upward at his daughter and felt a tear prickling at his eye.

Leonora, Strawbridge, and Madame Celeste had done their work well. But then, as Madame Celeste had said, with such beauty as Miss Hobart's, little work needed to be done.

Tripping lightly down the stairs on little white slippers, she was a radiant vision of youth and grace, all that a young girl should be on her presentation night.

Her blond hair had been simply dressed, with only a few curls falling about her face, a coronet of white rosebuds resting about her crown.

Her gown was simplicity itself, a white silk open robe embroidered with seashells and net, trimmed in a simple rouleau of white satin, opening to reveal a satin underskirt trimmed in pointe-de-Venise lace, wadded at the hem and trimmed with three more satin rouleaux, each one caught with a padded scallop of white taffeta.

Over her arms Strawbridge had draped a spiderweb-gauze shawl shot with silver pointes, and she carried a small white nosegay of rosebuds. Tiny pearls dropped from her ears, and upon one wrist she wore a bracelet of seed pearls clasped with pavé diamonds in the shape of a scallop shell.

"Well, Papa, how do I look?" she asked a little breathlessly, turning about for his inspection.

Sir Julian felt a lump in his throat as he embraced his daughter. "Beautiful," he said. "Just beautiful. Your mother would have been so proud of you."

"Oh, I would hope so, Papa," Jane sighed.

He cleared his throat, patting her shoulder. "There, there! Almost forgetting!" From an interior pocket he withdrew a velvet case, handing it to his daughter. "Little gift!"

She opened it eagerly, withdrawing a strand of matched pearls. "Oh, Papa!" she breathed, quite forgetting herself as she crushed against him in a hug. "Thank you! Thank you!"

Sir Julian looked above her head to see Lady Leonora Ware, just turned out of the hands of Strawbridge, paused to look down at them, a smile playing about her face, a gloved hand resting on the balcony railing.

"Ah, Lady Leonora!" he called. "Come and help me with this clasp, if you please! Never was much good with women's things!"

"As you wish," Leonora said evenly, quite certain that Sir Julian had clasped more than one piece of jewelry about the neck of some fair lady, in his time.

"Another vision!" he exclaimed as she stepped into the light.

For herself, Leonora had chosen a ball gown of ivory-and-claret-striped satin, cut low to the bodice and trimmed with Vandyke lace. The claret sleeves were slashed and mitered to reveal ivory satin beneath, lozenged with claret and caught with tiny corsages of silk. Her deeply embroidered hem was cut in three tiers of Vandyke lace, each draped to reveal a layer of ivory satin covered in lace-of-Parma. About her neck she had clasped a necklace of glittering diamonds, and upon her hair, dressed *à la Meduse*, she wore a small diadem of the same diamonds tremblant upon tiny platinum stems. Diamonds dropped from her ears, and a thin band of that jewel was clasped about one wrist.

If Jane was breathtaking in her innocence and beauty, Leonora was all that a sophisticated female of fashion should be.

"My compliments, ma'am!" Sir Julian said admiringly. "You are most lovely this evening. And my thanks for what you have done for my Jane!"

Leonora laughed and snapped her fan flirtatiously. "La, sir, as my grandmother used to say. Come, I think our first guests are arriving!"

The dinner for thirty-five couples, their most intimate friends, was all that Leonora could have wished it to be.

Since it was a notorious fact that there was not a decent piece of meat to be had in Vienna, the resourceful René had scoured the outlying countryside, and they dined wonderfully upon lamb, venison, wild duck, quail, and fish, together with several wonderful sauces, soups of mushroom and asparagus, four kinds of wine procured from heaven knew what source, for they were French and very good, and last, just the sort of rich sweet that Vienna was notorious for creating, a sort of *bombe Richelieu* filled with cream and chocolate that melted in the mouth.

It was obvious, Leonora thought, that no one would rise from the table hungry. She only hoped that they would not fall asleep on the dance floor.

Here again, René had outdone himself. By working closely with the fashionable decorator Moreau, he had managed to turn the cavernous, dank ballroom into a fantasy of a pleasure garden. The damp walls had been draped with white silk, and the peeling frescoes on the ceiling had been covered with a tent of flowers. Indeed, there were fresh flowers everywhere, although how or where Moreau and René had managed to procure them, Leonora would never know, nor did she think it wise to ask, since the only greenhouses in Vienna belonged to the Hofburg Palace. The dingy floor had been washed and waxed until it gleamed, and delicate French ballroom chairs, borrowed from Princess Bagration, stood clustered about in the corners.

The blue and yellow salons had been set up with card tables for those who preferred whist to dancing, and a light burned discreetly in the library for those who wished to settle a treaty or decide the question of the Rhine. Leonora hoped against hope that politics would not be a part of Jane's coming out, but she had also become wise enough to realize that it was inevitable that someone would confront someone else about something, for that was Vienna.

As the orchestra struck up the first dance, the obligatory polonaise, and Sir Julian led his daughter out on the floor, she could not help but feel a little lump in her throat, and was forced to dig in her reticule for her handkerchief.

"Allow me to help you," said a voice, and she turned to see Umberto, darkly handsome in his corbeau evening dress, grinning down at her as he offered his own handkerchief.

"Thank you," she said, genteelly blowing her nose.

"It would seem, Lady Leonora, that you have every right to shed a tear or two tonight. Jane is lovely. She will shine at this Congress. And it is all due to your efforts."

In spite of herself, Leonora smiled. "Do I hear a compliment?" she asked.

"You do, ma'am," Umberto replied easily. He looked at her dance card. "Do you have a place for me? . . . But you have no one!"

"Isn't it dreadful? I haven't had the time," she admitted.

"Then you must dance with me, if you please," Umberto said firmly, leading her out onto the floor, which was filling with other dancers.

He danced well and gracefully, leading her so slightly that she felt she might be dancing on air as he smiled down at her. "I hear you are a leading hostess now, and an invitation to your dinners is as much sought after as one to Countess Périgord's."

"Is that what you hear?" she asked lightly. "Then you must come! We see very little of you these days, you know. But I suppose Princess

Bagration keeps you busy," she added, just a little maliciously.

"She keeps everyone busy!" Umberto said lightly. "And who has been keeping you busy?"

"Jane!" Lady Leonora replied instantly. "Lord, I shall be glad when she is fixed with some nice young man."

"So, I think, will Sir Julian."

She threw him a sharp look, but said nothing, determined not to let him get to her.

"I suppose there is always a great deal of interest happening in the princess's apartments?"

"More than you could imagine. One drinks endless cups of tea and discusses politics and intrigues."

"How interesting."

"Very. I must say that the bits and pieces you have related to Julian have been quite interesting to us."

"I fear I am a very bad amateur spy, Umberto. No one ever tells me anything *interesting*. Although this really unspeakable baron did try to trap me in a corner at Metternich's and try to kiss me. I was forced to plant him a facer, as my brothers used to say, with my reticule."

Umberto laughed. "You are the most complete hand, my lady!"

"I get by," she admitted.

The music ended and they applauded politely. At that moment Leonora was claimed by Sir Charles Stewart, and did not see Umberto for the rest of the evening.

The night passed in a whirl. Prince Metternich, all medals and charm, danced with her and begged her to bring Miss Hobart to meet his own daughter, who was exactly her age. Lord Castlereagh claimed a waltz, which he performed with more gusto than style. The czar, who she suspected was a trifle foxed, danced a country dance with her, and told her that Castlereagh was a stubborn pig on the issue of Poland, among other things. She whirled about the floor in the arms of Sir Julian, and could not help but note that his attention was on another lady the entire time. She danced with young Count Zichy, husband of the lovely Julie, and he told her a very funny story about a donkey, a farmer, and a baker.

She greeted the Emperor and Empress of Austria, and presented Jane to them, before tactfully suggesting that what they might like would be a game of whist, and finding them partners, a bottle of champagne, and a quiet room where no one would bother them.

She sat for a while with Talleyrand, whose deformed foot prevented him from dancing, and they drank a glass of champagne and spoke of Lord Byron, whose poetry and politics seemed to interest Talleyrand greatly that evening. Watching as his eyes followed Dorothea Talleyrand Périgord about the room, she realized that he was in love with his young mistress and wondered what the outcome would be. When Metternich came over and sat down with them, and the talk turned to politics, Leonora listened politely for a while, then excused herself.

Doubtless Sagan or Bagration would have

stayed and even entered the talk, but Leonora decided she had her limits.

Bagration was all over the dance floor in her low-cut dress, exposing quite a bit of that very ample bosom and never lacking for a partner, obviously enjoying herself immensely, particularly with the young and best-looking of the gentlemen present, but she waved cheerfully to Leonora as she whirled past.

Leonora frowned when she saw Jane dancing with the handsome Prince Adam. Somehow, she sensed danger there, although she was not quite certain why. The man seemed more interested in the liberation of Poland than females. Now, if only there were some dashing aide-de-camp to Wellington, or junior attaché of great promise . . .

At that moment her attention was claimed by the Duchess of Sagan, in pearls and lilac, and they settled upon a sofa for a comfortable coze.

Very soon they were joined by Countess Périgord, the duchess's younger sister, and the talk turned from the gentlemen in power to the fact that the ladies had only that which they could scheme and wrest from them. There would be no wars, and no endless conferences like this one, the Duchess declared passionately, if only women could stand on a truly equal footing with men. She was well known to be politically conservative, and her outburst surprised Leonora a great deal, but she was forced to admit to the truth of it.

It was true that they were all here, and that they exerted influence upon the course of affairs.

But their influence was through the bedroom and the ballroom and the dining room, rather than the conference table.

For a moment the three of them sat watching the ball.

Then Sagan shook the feathers in her headdress. "I do not know why it is supposed that women are less intelligent than men. In truth, we are far more clever than they will ever be, for circumstances have forced us to be so!"

"Perhaps, like the publishers and the German Jews, we should have sent a delegation hither," Dorothea Talleyrand Périgord suggested gravely, her enormous eyes serious.

"And that delegation would be treated like the publishers and Nathan Rothschild's delegation," the duchess said bitterly. "Ignored. Shunted aside. Ah! But I, for one, intend to do exactly as I please, and care not for what people may say of me!"

Since it was already well known that she was Metternich's mistress, Leonora wondered what else she *could* do.

Slowly, she looked from one sister to the other. The Courland princesses, known throughout Europe for beauty, wealth, breeding, and charm. They could have had anything they wanted, and these were the life-styles they had chosen for themselves in the end, to become the mistresses of powerful men. Truly, it was an odd world, even now changing into heaven only knew what by the time this Congress was over.

Wilhelmina Sagan laughed, shaking her lovely head. "But come! This is a ball! We do not need such serious talk tonight. A lovely young girl makes her debut, and one hopes that she will find a man she will love and be happy ever after!"

"One hopes," Leonora repeated.

The candles were guttering in their sockets and the thinnest red line of dawn was breaking by the time the last guest had left.

Exhausted, Leonora wanted only to get out of her stays and crawl into bed, but Jane, flying on excitement, could have talked forever, had not Strawbridge firmly put her out of the room.

"It is not at all what a good Englishwoman is used to," she announced, holding up Leonora's slippers to show that the soles had been danced clear through.

"No, it is not, is it?" Leonora yawned, pulling the counterpane over her head and instantly falling asleep.

11

THERE WAS A singularly unattractive gilt-and-porcelain clock on the marble mantelpiece of Lady Leonora's room that was chiming noon in a particularly grating way that finally awakened her from her deep sleep.

Try as she might, to go back into that blissful state was impossible, and with a moan, she rang for Strawbridge.

That female appeared instantly, her thin lips set in a line of disapproval. "Yes, my lady?" she asked.

"Coffee," Leonora gasped, and fell back among the pillows again. "No tea. Coffee."

Strawbridge disappeared in a rustle of gray merino, and Leonora tried very hard not to think about anything.

In due course, Jane, fresh and lively in sprigged muslin, and not Strawbridge, appeared, bearing a silver tray, which she placed on Leonora's lap.

"René says to drink this, and not to ask what its contents are. He says it will make you feel much more the thing."

As Jane watched, Leonora tasted it and made a face.

"René says to gulp it all down at once."

Leonora did as she was bid, holding her nose as she drained the glass. "God," she choked. "That was awful!"

"René says to drink too much champagne is deadly," Jane added, sitting down and regarding Lady Leonora cheerfully.

Opening one eye, Lady Leonora glared back at her. "Go away, do," she pleaded. "You don't want to see a grown female die, you know."

"Oh, you aren't going to die. You've got the blue devils. Anyway, there are all sorts of flowers and notes and things downstairs from the ball. We are a success!"

Leonora ventured to say where she thought all diplomats could be sent, and Jane shook her head.

"And Umberto came by this morning, with a wonderful bouquet of roses, and he says that no matter how blue-deviled you are, you must be dressed in your habit and ready by two, because he has a surprise for you."

"I don't want to know what it is," Leonora replied. "It sounds as if it involves moving about, and that I cannot stand." She opened one eye. "What is it?"

"It's a surprise, so of course I can't tell you, but oh, it is a bang-up bit of blood and bone as I have ever seen!"

"Jane, your use of cant is perfectly dreadful, and I don't know where you learn these things," Leonora moaned.

"That is what Lord Umberto said."

"He would. What else did he say?"

"Just that you must be up and dressed and ready by two." With that, Jane left the room, humming a waltz, off upon some mysterious Jane mission.

At two, Leonora, her blue devils partially exorcised, and attired in a very dashing hussar-style habit of blue broadcloth trimmed with gold frogs and braid, a red velvet toque tilted jauntily over one eyebrow, a set of good York tan gloves on her hands, and her sturdy riding boots upon her feet, descended the stairs to find Lord Umberto, his riding attire of his usual dark hues, awaiting her in the hallway.

"Ah, I see that I find you in one piece!" he announced jauntily, escorting her to the door, where a groom held two horses against the curb.

One was Umberto's black stallion; the other was a bay mare of good points and frisky energy, already bridled and sidesaddled.

"Oh, she *is* a bang-up piece of blood and bone!" Leonora exclaimed delightedly, approaching the mare with gentle words and a caressing stroke. "But wherever did you find her? There must not be a decent horse anywhere in Vienna that's not bought, rented, or borrowed!"

"Well, it took a little doing, but I found her at last. She has some German name I cannot pronounce, but if you will address her as Gretel, that will do well enough, I think."

Leonora ran her hand over the horse's withers. "She's a beauty!"

"Then up you go!" Umberto boosted her into the saddle, and Leonora took the reins, pacing the high-stepping mare up and down the cobblestones, exclaiming with delight at the way in which the mare responded.

"It seems forever since I have been on a horse," she said. "But oh, it feels so good to ride again!"

"I am glad you feel that way, for you and I are going off upon an adventure for the afternoon," Umberto said, swinging himself easily into the stallion's saddle.

Leonora glanced across at him. "An adventure? I think I have had enough of those for a while!"

"Ah, but I think that you will enjoy this one. The day is lovely, the air clear and brisk, and the path we go not terribly difficult. Although I regret to say it is not a well-traveled road."

"Don't tease me, Umberto, for you know I dislike that above all things. Where do we go?"

"A lovely palace, out of a fairy tale, on the outskirts of Vienna, called the Schönbrunn, where a very lovely lady lives."

Another one of his *chères amies*, Leonora thought, but said nothing, giving herself over to the beauty of the day, the pleasure of riding again, and the changing streets of Vienna as they approached the ancient ramparts that marked the edge of the city.

As they rode along, they talked but little, comfortable with silence as two friends can be. A good horsewoman, Leonora was occupied with learning the tricks of her mount, and the moment they had left the city walls, she could not resist breaking into a most unladylike gallop across the countryside.

Umberto kept up with her easily enough on his big mount, and from time to time they each threw a smile at the other, a smile of perfect understanding.

Wild-haired and disheveled, she was unprepared for the enormous edifice she saw when she mounted the rise, and she reined in her horse, looking at it gleaming golden in the afternoon sunshine.

"The Schönbrunn," Umberto said simply.

It was as Umberto had said, a fairytale palace, like something from one of the books she had read as a child. It was not, as she had first thought, gold, but painted a yellow that caught the reflection of the sunlight with the glimmer of gold. All baroque curlicues and swirls, galleries and curved windows, it sat in the middle of its own large park of horse-chestnut trees, dreaming and enchanted.

As they rode up the drive, Leonora felt a curious silence about the place, as if it had been put beneath the spell of a sleeping beauty, to awaken in a hundred years.

The eerie feeling of timelessness was suddenly and joyfully broken when a very small boy darted from one of the gravel paths after a runaway hoop.

With a shout, Umberto dismounted, and the little boy came running toward him, adorable to Leonora in his one-piece suit with his enormous dark eyes. Formally, he made a small bow to Umberto, who in return bowed even deeper before gravely shaking his hand. They spoke in German, and Leonora could not understand what was being said, but in a moment a very tall woman in a round dress of red and gold came from the same path, carrying her hat in her hand. Again Umberto bowed, and the woman, not much older than Jane, returned his bow with one of her own, grave and dignified. She spoke to him in rapid German mixed with French, and as she spoke, she held the little boy close to her skirts, listening intently to Umberto's reply, before shaking her head and making a gesture of despair or impatience.

Whatever he had told her, she seemed resigned, if not pleased. She shook his hand, and the little boy waved. Umberto bowed, and the woman and child turned slowly away, walking down the path from which they had come.

He strode back toward Leonora, mounting his horse. "Forgive me, Lady Leonora, I know I should have introduced you, but at present such introductions are awkward. The lady is Marie Louise, daughter of the Austrian emperor and wife of the former French emperor, and her son, who was the King of Rome."

Leonora looked down the path at the retreating figures.

"The Austrian emperor has Marie Louise and her son housed here until the Congress decides who and what they are. It is very difficult for her, as you can imagine. She is neither fish nor fowl, nor is her son one thing or another. She leads a lonely life, for no one ever comes to visit her, and she is surrounded by her French staff. She is even separated from her particular friend Count von Neipperg."

"It is very sad," Leonora said quietly. "She has done nothing to deserve this!"

"Tell the rest of the world that," Umberto replied.

"Then why do you see her?" Leonora asked after a while as they were riding along.

Umberto grinned. "Because Neipperg is a friend of mine, and he asked me to bring her a message of hope. You see, ma'am, I am not totally without heart."

Beneath her hat, Leonora smiled. "Not totally," she agreed.

On their way back to Vienna, they stopped at a charming little inn called the Neuplatz, an ancient timbered and stuccoed building of many gables and turns, where ivy grew up the old walls, and the yards were filled with the blooming flowers of late autumn, bursting forth in the colors of flame. The landlord, a large jovial man with a hussar's mustache and a spotless white apron stretched across his bulging middle, greeted Lord Umberto effusively, making a low and courtly bow over Lady Leonora's hand as he sent for his apple-cheeked daughter to see to her needs. His wife came rushing from the kitchen still drying her hands on a towel, crying her greetings to Lord Umberto and making her curtsy to his lady companion. It was very clear that he was an old and valued guest here, for a table was laid with a gleaming linen cloth beneath the striped awning on the terrace overlooking the Danube in the distance, and Herr Guttmann personally supervised their meal. The fare was simple but delicious. There were good spiced sausages and ripe, tangy cheeses, loaves of brown bread with crisp crusts still warm from the oven, yellow butter and sharp pot cheese, sharp and juicy red and yellow apples, and mellow ales that tasted of autumn, followed by coffee with heavy whipped cream and layered pastries so delicate that they seemed to melt upon the tongue.

They ate ravenously, for the day's ride had made them hungry, and spoke but little, concentrating on the food.

Nothing, it would seem, would please the Guttmanns more than a hearty appetite, for they nodded with approval with each dish that was returned empty, until at last Leonora placed her napkin upon the table declaring one more morsel would make her burst.

Umberto suggested that a stroll would work it all off, and they wandered comfortably down the paths through the meadows of grazing sheep toward the winding blue river, where they sat down upon a turnlock, contemplating the lazy flow of the water through the weeds.

"One does not like to sound like a traveler,

but it could almost be England," Leonora said thoughtfully, propping her chin in her hand.

"One could almost be homesick," Umberto agreed, picking a straw and chewing it between his teeth. "For the salmon and the wildweed and the hedgerows."

"Almost, but not quite," Leonora replied. "I wonder that I never dreamed of travel when I was a girl. I suppose because of the wars. And now that one has, one wants to keep on forever and ever."

"Journeys end in lovers' meetings." Umberto tossed a stone into the water. It skipped before it sank. "My nanny used to say that. I wonder if it is true."

"I do not know," Leonora said, gathering her skirts. "Certainly they seem to do so for the Princess Bagration."

"I wonder if this journey shall end thus for Lady Leonora Ware," Umberto mused, chewing at his grass and squinting thoughtfully into the sun.

"I rather doubt it," Lady Leonra said lightly. "I have no heart, recall."

Umberto touched her hand lightly, then slid his arm easily about her shoulders. She did not resist, but laid her head against his shoulder, feeling a trifle giddy. "Ah, but do you know? I have begun to believe that there is something in the air of Vienna that has made that lady's heart awaken. I feel it stirring faintly beneath that fashionable exterior; that romantic girl still breathes."

Leonora, discomfited a little, moved away,

recalling who she was, who Umberto was, and why she believed they could never be anything more than mere friends, even in Vienna.

"Do you notice, Umberto, that it grows dark?" she asked a little breathlessly, drawing on her gloves. "Perhaps we should start back."

Before he could protest, she had begun to walk up the path. Umberto pushed a hand through his dark hair, shaking his head ruefully. Slowly he rose to his own feet and cast away his straw, pushing his hands into his pockets as he followed her.

After a cool and restrained ride back to the city, Leonora arrived home to find that there was no time to think about Umberto, for the house was in a state of crisis. Sir Julian, still in his shirtsleeves, was pacing about, and Jane, ravishing in pink gauze, was near tears.

"I forbid it!" Sir Julian was saying, peering beneath the furniture for a lost collar button. "I absolutely forbid it! No daughter of mine will ever, under any circumstances, enter that house! Particularly, miss, under those circumstances! I tell you, it would be no better than a Covent Garden Mask, and what sort of father would I be to allow you to attend a Covent Garden Mask, hey?"

"Everyone else is going!" Jane protested. "Julie Zichy, Marie Metternich!"

"If Laure Metternich is mad enough to allow her daughter to attend such an affair, then I wonder for her! Countess Zichy is a married lady, and under the protection of her husband!

But you, young lady, are a properly brought-up Englishwoman, and I say no!"

Sir Julian, half in and half out of his coat, stooped and peered beneath a dresser while Chandler fumbled with his cravat, clearly embarrassed. In a corner, Miss Strawbridge searched the sofa cushions, muttering that it was not at all what a good Englishwoman was used to, and René, his face expressionless, ran a finger along the mantel.

"What in the world . . . ?" Leonora asked, drawing off her bonnet and gloves, and several persons stopped what they were doing and looked at her.

"Sir Julian's collar button—"

"Good evening, madam, it would seem—"

"Lady Leonora, *tell* him!"

"Thank God! Lady Leonora! Now we may be put to rights!"

Exhausted and redolent of horse, Leonora sank into a chair and looked about herself.

"Princess Bagration is having a costume ball," Jane began breathlessly. "It is going to be *the* affair of the season. And we are all invited, including me!"

"The light begins to dawn," Leonora said.

"And of course she's not going! I won't have my daughter at one of the Bagration's *orgies!*" Sir Julian exclaimed.

"What's a orgies?" Jane asked.

"There you have it," Sir Julian said firmly.

"But Marie Metternich is going! And Julie Zichy!" Jane exclaimed heatedly.

"I find it hard to believe that Laure Metternich would allow her daughter to attend a costume ball at the princess's," Leonora said.

"Well, at least she's allowed to go if I'm allowed to go," Jane admitted.

"Ah," Leonora nodded. "I see. Well, I shall speak with Madam Metternich, and see what we shall decide. In the meantime, you will be content with that, my dear."

"There we have it! There we have it!" Sir Julian said, much relieved. "Knew that you could be counted on, ma'am!" He shook his head. "Not good at this debbing and mothering, not good at all!"

Jane sniffed eloquently and flounced out of the room.

"Come, Strawbridge, I must dress, or we shall all be late," Leonora sighed, rising from her seat.

"*Une autre crise domestique relevé,*" René murmured, holding up the collar button.

Tonight it was a dinner at Talleyrand's, or as Sir Julian complained in the carriage, a squeeze of overheated people in overheated rooms, overdressed, overlooked, overfed, and overentertained by Mlle. Grassi, the opera singer whose high notes periodically awakened him from his postprandial slumbers.

Dorothea was of course lovely and charming and beautifully turned out in celestial blue, and Talleyrand his usual sardonic self, seeing everything and missing nothing as he limped from group to group, smiling a smile that never quite reached his eyes.

Leonora vowed that should he tell her he

had been to see Marie Louise and had received a proposal of something from that lady, she would start pulling his medals from his tunic one by one, but fortunately for him, he confined his conversation with her to the most trivial pleasantries concerning Jane's ball, where, he said, he had enjoyed himself greatly, and had won a handsome sum from the czar at cards.

Jane drifted about the room, arm in arm with Marie Metternich, and Leonora was certain they were both aware of the admiring looks they were receiving from all the young gentlemen present. She was rather glad that the handsome Polish prince was nowhere to be seen.

If she was disappointed that Lord Umberto was also absent, she was relieved to note that the Castlereaghs were nowhere in attendance either, meaning business at the legation.

Hopefully, that business did not include Princess Bagration, for she did feel relieved when that lady drifted in after dinner—all shawls, bosom, and jewels—on the arm of a handsome Russian hussar named Serge, who smiled a great deal and said very little, but drank copious amounts. Rather cattily, Leonora supposed he had to, given his duties. Of course, she regretted the thought and sat upon the sofa and chatted with the princess for a space of time, learning that the czar was being a very naughty boy, that cashmere shawls could be had on Johannesplatz for forty pounds sterling, that Sagan was furious with Metternich for spending so much time with his wife and family, that Isabey had almost completed her portrait, that her stepfather had sent her some money and a Russian fortune teller who nearly always told the truth, and that her Bal Masque was going to be the Major Event of Next Week, since everyone in Vienna was invited.

As always when talking to Bagration, Leonora felt out of breath without saying a word. The princess was simply a force of nature, like the wind or the rain, and whatever her faults, it was impossible not to like her, for she was possessed of both generosity and charm. "Both of which can be deadly," Leonora thought that she heard Umberto saying in her mind, but she shrugged it off. If she could but be like Catherine Bagration and take lovers as one might buy a hat, then perhaps she might have Umberto. But Leonora was incapable of such behavior. She shook her sadness off and smiled, listening to the princess describing her plans for the Bal Masque.

Certainly it sounded like a great deal of amusement, and it would seem that there was nothing that could be considered objectionable for a young girl with common sense and a proper upbringing. Jane had common sense, and certainly knew how to depress the pretensions of an encroaching suitor in no uncertain terms. Certainly she knew to avoid situations that might lead to trouble. Besides, both Sir Julian and Lady Leonora would be there to keep an eye on her. Although, Leonora thought, it had begun to seem to her that Sir Julian simply liked to keep an eye on any attractive female who came his way.

When she happened, later in the evening, to encounter the gentle and soft-spoken Laure Metternich, Leonora broached the situation with her, and the princess agreed that as long as both girls were chaperoned, there could be no objection to their attendance. Marie Metternich was her father's favorite child, and he was certain not to allow her to escape his eye all evening. "Besides, Lady Leonora," the princess added, "if they become too high-spirited, we may always take them home!"

Having agreed, Princess Metternich and Lady Leonora planned to meet later in the week to work out the details of costume, both certain the girls would insist upon something far more outrageous than would be appropriate. But there would be more masked balls before the Congress was over, and they thought it wise to expose them to one now, rather than later.

The following week was a busy one for Lady Leonora, and she did not have more than a few hours here and there to think about Umberto, although a wistful feeling seemed to have penetrated her entire being, much to her own annoyance.

In the end, Sir Julian had prevailed, and both Leonora and Jane dutifully went off each morning after breakfast to the Jungenstrassen-platz, where they undraped their shoulders in the freezing cold and harsh light of the studio of Isabey, the highly fashionable portrait painter, in order that they might be among the fashionable females captured by his brush.

Leonora, who loved her straightforward and no-nonsense Lawrence, was a little uncertain about Isabey, however fashionable he might be. She found herself posed, bare-shouldered and embarrassingly décolleté, in a cloud of spiderweb gauze and ruffled shawls, her hair tangled into a morass of curls and ribbons and rosebuds, her head tilted upward, eyes wide, nose lengthened, lips parted with an expression so vacuous and pseudo-spiritual, all seeming to have been perceived by the painter through a veil of cheese-cloth, that she privately thought she looked more like a rather stupid spaniel than a woman of enough age and experience to avoid romantic pretensions toward a youth and innocence she had long ago left behind her.

That women twice her age and lacking good looks were clamoring to have their likenesses done in such a manner made her sad.

The restless Jane, who could never sit still for more than a quarter-hour, however, was Isabey's greatest delight. Here he need not remove two or three extra chins, or straighten the hook in a nose. She was in herself perfection, and he need only plead with her from time to time to please stop fidgeting for just a little while.

Fortunately, Isabey had a great store of *on-dits*, and he was able to use these to keep Jane entertained for long stretches of time, although Leonora sometimes cleared her throat to warn him that he was veering into the slightly off-color.

But when he had finished, he threw down his brushes and declared that he could do no better ever again, and even though Leonora thought it artistic exaggeration, she was pleased with his work.

He had caught Jane looking out at the viewer from a slight angle, a tiny smile on her lips and that mischievous sparkle in her eyes that Leonora found one of her most attractive characteristics. Her blond hair had been simply dressed, with only one or two curls before her ears and a careless Psyche knot atop her crown, but she needed no elaborate hairstyles to compliment her loveliness. Her shoulders gently sloped into the open neckline of her simple white silk round dress, and one hand, resting against her breast, played with her rope of pearls. It was simplicity itself, and it said all that there was to say about Miss Jane Hobart, caught at the first flush of her beauty at the age of eighteen.

"Well, now," Sir Julian said, when it was framed and hung in the Yellow Saloon, "That's something more like, what?"

To Lady Leonora he whispered later, "Cost me every bit of eight hundred pounds, but it's worth it. It's worth it."

She had to agree that it was, although when Lord Umberto came to dine one evening and looked at her own, he merely shook his head. "Makes you look like a sad spaniel, you know," he said quite seriously. "I'd like to see you painted by David, I think. He would be your man."

Lady Leonora, torn between exasperation at his bluntness and amusement at the thought that he had echoed her thoughts exactly, only looked at him and moved away to greet the King of Denmark. Nor did she speak or smile at him through the rest of dinner, a rather dull affair for all the parties involved in the attempt to achieve an international copyright agreement.

Leonora did, however, wish that she could pull her turban down over her flaming face and stuff a damask napkin into her mouth when, toward the end of the meal, Umberto stood up, holding his glass aloft, and said, "Ladies and gentlemen! I give you . . . Napoleon!"

There was an audible gasp about the room, and more than one lady fanned herself.

"I grant you," Lord Umberto said, "that he was the monster of Europe, and that Elba is not yet far enough away from here! But, ladies and gentlemen, Napoleon Bonaparte once shot a publisher!"

Leonora breathed a sigh of relief as the laughter began to peal out across the board, and she actually saw a publisher, reduced to tears of laughter, slap an author upon the back. Sir Julian was rolling in his chair, shaking his head from side to side.

What had been a dull and routine dinner suddenly came alive, and a female from Denmark who specialized in English-Danish translations, began to tell a story about certain language difficulties she had experienced, communicating with Byron's editor. The climax of the story was so funny that everyone roared again.

By the time that the fruit and cheese were served, no one dreamed that the ladies should follow the custom of withdrawing, leaving the men to their port and cigars. Serious progress was being made, compromises were being worked out, and several people had come to the point of taking out their gold pencil cases to make notes of agreement on the damask napkins.

It was not, Leonora thought, an enormous cog in the grander scheme of the Congress, but *something* that would affect a great many people had happened, and at her dinner table tonight, things had been accomplished.

In an excusably self-congratulatory mood, she felt as if she had played a minor part in helping the Congress to work.

At that moment Umberto happened to catch her eye, with a cigarillo clutched between his teeth, grinning at her as if he were reading her thoughts.

A little stab of pain clutched at her heart, and she was surprised to find herself owning to being in possession of one of those most interesting organs.

If only things were different, she thought. If only there had never been a Richard to stand between them! Umberto was completely mad, totally impossible, incredibly odious, and the most wonderful man she had ever known.

She shook her head, as if to clear her mind. Vienna was only a few weeks of magic and power, after all, a heady intoxication that she would only dimly recall when she was at home in London, something that had come together and was then forgotten, just as she must surely forget her feelings for Umberto.

12

"CHANDLER! CHANDLER! DAMN, where is the fella?" Sir Julian bellowed angrily, stalking out of his dressing room. "Chandler!" he roared over the stair rail, and two maids and a footman suddenly made themselves disappear, trembling in their dark hiding places.

"Sir Julian, if there were any dead in this house, and I do not really want to question that too closely, you would be shouting loud enough to wake them!" Tying her embroidered dressing gown about her waist, Lady Leonora emerged from the Rose Room, a white mobcap over her curl papers and an anxious Strawbridge trailing behind with the curling tongs, looking upward at Sir Julian as if he were a naughty schoolboy.

"I just want to know if I am supposed to wear this . . . this thingamabob to this damned party tonight," he answered rather plaintively, holding up a shapeless black garment lined with red silk. "Bad enough I've got to go to the damn thing in the first place, but tell me, ma'am, *what in hell is this thing?*"

"That is the cape, of course," Leonora replied calmly. "You are going as what you are. A Renaissance gentleman. Chandler is belowstairs pressing out the rest of the costume."

Sir Julian's chest puffed out a little, and his spirits seemed to take a little turn for the better. "Renaissance sort of fella, hey? Is that how you see me?"

"That is the way in which Jane perceives you, Sir Julian, and a very flattering thought it is, also," Leonora assured him. "Now, you go and wait, and Chandler will bring the rest of it up directly. You will look very dashing, I assure you!"

"Oh, very well," Sir Julian sighed. "Damn La Bagration and her crack-brained parties anyway. Haven't had one night to put my feet up on my own grate since I got to Vienna. . . ." His voice trailed away as he closed his door.

Leonora sighed. "I suppose that is half the battle," she told Strawbridge. "But wait until he sees the doublet and hose. Jane will have to deal with that."

"It is not at all what a good Englishwoman is used to," Strawbridge said direfully, closing Lady Leonora's door behind her.

Within the hour, Leonora's door opened again, and a Tudor lady, complete to ruff and farthingale, emerged not without some difficulty managing that farthingale through the doorway. Her hair was covered by her peaked cap and veil, and she wore a black silk mask over her eyes and face. Strawbridge, still brushing at the velvet, followed behind, fussing.

Never having worn but one hoop in her life, and that for her presentation at court, Leonora took the staircase warily, wondering how they managed it day in and day out, but she arrived at the bottom in one piece, with a modicum of grace, and was surprised when she almost tripped over René and Jane sitting on the last step.

"Well, how do I do?" she asked, untying her mask.

René nodded. "You look very much like Lady Lettice Ware on the grand staircase at home," he said, pacing all about her, his arms behind his back, checking her over critically. "Only perhaps not so sad," he added, with a glance at Jane that Leonora did not see.

"That was my idea, René. To look like Lettice. I always loved those Tudor costumes."

"Take care you do not meet her fate," René said lightly.

"What was her fate?" asked Jane curiously.

"Her lover kidnapped her and took her to France, where we think that he beat her and drank away all their money."

"*Moi*, I think they lived happily ever after, and drank wine and ate Anjou pears," René said lightly. "And now, if you please," he announced, removing the evening cloak Jane had been wearing, "La Belle Jeune Fille de l'Ancien Régime!"

Jane had dressed as one of Marie Antoinette's *jeunes filles* who played at being shepherdesses at Le Petit Trianon. Her blond hair was powdered lightly, and piled beneath a chipstraw bonnet fastened beneath her chin with a broad pink ribbon, and tied beneath one ear in a charming bow. A corsage of silk daisies was perched rakishly upon the crown, and it was trimmed with a thin edge of lace.

Her dress was of the old style, pink-and-white-striped silk, cut low and filled with a lacy fichu knotted at the breast. The bodice and waist were cut tight to the figure, and laced over a white silk stomacher. Likewise, the sleeves were tight to the elbow, then flared outward in a mass of lace.

The full skirt, supported by six or seven full petticoats beneath, ended above the clocks in her stockings, and all about the hem, the lacy petticoats flared out prettily, swirling as she walked. Upon her feet she wore high-heeled satin shoes with the red heels of the aristocracy, clasped with rhinestone buckles. In one hand she carried a dearly silly little shepherdess's crook, painted pink and trimmed with silk flowers and ribbons.

"You look utterly charming, my dear," Leonora said. "Every young man there tonight will wonder who you are, and fall in love."

"Oh, I mean to break hearts," Jane giggled. "If I don't break an ankle first. These heels are not at all what one is used to wearing."

"This is what I recall from my childhood," René said simply, gesturing toward Jane. "Gone. All gone forever."

"Except for tonight, René," Jane said softly, laying an easy hand upon his arm. "Tonight, it is all here again."

"*Oui*," he agreed. "*Mais, plus ça change, plus c'est la même chose*. Louise le Cochon is back on his throne, *mais ce n'est pas le même chose du tout*. Antoinette was Austrian, you know. . . ." His voice trailed off and he shrugged. "Who knows what will happen here, if anything? It is all a play, and we are all the actors with our little parts to play. Tonight, *ma chère* Jane, you go out for me, *tu comprends?*"

"*Oui*," she said seriously.

"Great bloody pack of fools we shall all be tonight," Sir Julian grumbled as he clomped down the stairs. "Probably Catherine's idea of playing some great joke on us all!"

But neither his daughter nor his hostess could find fault with his costume, that of a gentleman of the Italian Renaissance. He had an excellent leg, and filled out his doublet and hose to admiration, they declared, without need of padding or corset. His figure was trim and displayed well in his tunic, and the velvet cap seated on his blond locks made him look rakishly dashing, just as he ought, like a Sforza prince.

Even these assurances from his womenfolk did not completely reassure him that he was not making the biggest cake in nature of himself, and he informed René most balefully that if he dared to open his mouth, Sir Julian would be forced to call him a countercoxcomb and a great many other appellations he would regret.

René raised a brow, but said nothing, saving his thoughts on the subject for the friend whose genius ruled the kitchen.

Thus, the party departed in their carriage

for the Palm Palace. As their carriage was awaiting its turn to deposit them at the door, Leonora
was interested to note that while Bagration's side
positively seemed on fire with light, the Duchess
of Sagan's, on the right side of the building, was
as dark as a tomb.

Bagration, Leonora noticed as their hostess
greeted them at the top of the stairs, had, as
usual, outdone herself. Leonora assumed that
the princess was supposed to be Cleopatra, for
she wore a sort of Egyptian-looking tiara, featuring a bronze snake, in her dark hair, and a
great deal of Egyptian-looking necklaces, rings,
bracelets, anklets, toe rings, and earrings, but
there was really very little else at all to her
costume save some sort of piece of pleated gauze
that had been dampened and wrapped about
her very luscious form, of which one could see,
without straining, every charm.

For some reason, Leonora wanted to laugh,
for after all, it was just Bagration being Bagration
again, but she really did have to pinch Jane's
arm very hard to stir her out of her trance and
force her to make her curtsy to her hostess.

As she passed on into the ballroom, she
noticed that Sir Julian was certainly enjoying it
all, and wondered why, since there was nothing
there he had not seen before.

As Jane and Leonora entered the archways,
they paused, both of them struck by the sheer
number of cavorting costumed guests. Whatever
people might say about the princess, no one ever
missed one of her parties, for she knew how to
entertain well and lavishly. The room had been

done in an Egyptian theme, draped in cloth of gold and covered with what Leonora supposed were meant to represent hieroglyphs and artifacts along the Nile. She would not have been surprised if Catherine had begged or borrowed the sphinx itself to place in the middle of the room, but she seemed to have settled for—or perhaps the fashionable decorator Moreau had made do with—decorated columns, pyramids offering seats, and yes! sphinxes pouring forth fountains of the very best champagne. Even the orchestra had been decked out in Egyptian rig, and very unhappy they looked about it, too, sawing away at a waltz wearing the headdresses of the pharaohs.

Amid all of these interesting things, costumed and masked dancers whirled about the floor or intrigued in the corners.

Already overwhelmed by the decor, it took Leonora a moment to recall how very disorienting it can be to come into a room of people who are not what they should be, but disguised as something else. And it was only then that she recalled what great license mask and costume seem to grant those who would never dream of acting with anything but the greatest propriety when in their own clothing. She worried not for herself, but for Jane, thinking of that story about the Russian hussar and the little Viennese girl he had tried to attack in these very rooms.

She turned toward Jane, and realized she was gone. For a moment Leonora felt a sense of panic, casting wildly about for Sir Julian, but then she caught sight of that pink-and-white shepherdess making her way toward a medieval princess in lavender and white wearing a little necklace that she recognized as Marie Metternich's, and she relaxed, castigating herself for being a great silly. The two of them were inexorably swallowed up in a swarm of young men so obviously from the various delegations, all of them pressing to put their names on a dance card or procure a glass of champagne.

Across the room she saw Metternich, far too dignified to disguise himself with anything more than a silk domino, glancing toward his daughter from time to time, and she sighed with relief, fanning herself furiously.

A corsair in turban and sword bowed and asked in a heavy Italian accent if she wished to dance, and Leonora allowed herself to be led out on the floor, where she moved easily through a Viennese country dance.

The corsair gave way to a Scot, whose build and tartan so obviously identified him as Sir Charles Stewart that she knew him at once, and teased him about it quite dreadfully until he recognized her by her voice. Then she was claimed by someone she thought might be a parrot, so feathered was his costume, and so clumsy was he on his feet that she was relieved to be claimed by a very handsome Gypsy from the Russian delegation, who complimented her far too lavishly on any part of her body that he could see and wanted to know if she would meet him somewhere later. She suspected he was very foxed and named a place that did not exist, suspecting twenty women had already done the same thing that night, if only to rid themselves of such an odious creature without creating an ugly scene.

The Russian holy man was so obvious that he made Charles Stewart look subtle. And subtle was something Charles Stewart would never, ever be. "We waltz yet again, sir," she said to the czar, who really was a very good dancer, she thought, having had several glasses of champagne.

"We waltz yet again," he repeated, thinking this over. "But I waltz with everyone except my wife. The black-and-white dress, the style of the English Henry. The voice, English also, and the pearl-and-diamond necklace. Hmmm. Lady Leonora Ware, my charming hostess at Miss Hobart's ball! How do you go on? I do not see you for many days, a week perhaps. You do not go to state dinner at Hofburg last night?"

"Alas, no. I hosted a very dull but very successful meeting-dinner concerning international copyright of books!"

The czar clicked his tongue. "How very dull for you when you could have been dancing or gossiping or attending some fashionable event."

"No, sir. I was glad I was there. I helped to accomplish something, however insignificant it might have been to anyone but a publisher of books."

"You have a serious side, Lady Leonora. That is interesting. Perhaps we should have you at the Chancellery to help us."

"Perhaps you all ought to come and eat dinner with us. We are rather informal, you know, which people seem to enjoy." She paused. "But you know what you ought to do is keep your soldiers from getting so foxed! It is very annoying!"

"Bonaparte said an army travels on its stomach. I say an army travels on good Russian vodka. But my cousin Bagration invited none of my soldiers here tonight. Only *important* people. Not even more than one or two generals, and they know better than to get drunk at a ball. That's why they are generals."

"There is a Russian hussar here, Czar, dressed as a Gypsy, who is quite foxed," Leonora insisted. "Perhaps he sneaked in."

"Perhaps he is one of my cousin's . . . er, friends. In which case, he would do well not to be too drunk. She is not a lady to take disappointment well." He laughed, winking at Leonora behind his mask. "She *throws* things," he confided.

Fortunately for Leonora, the dance ended, and she only needed applaud and drop a small curtsy to royalty, who was already wandering away in search of another pretty woman. Leonora could never quite comprehend the czar's attraction to her, particularly since he was making trouble for the English at the conferences and had said, after his London visit, that British women were ill-mannered and ugly. The same, she thought, might be said about the czar's favorite sister, Grand Duchess Catherine, for whom she had taken an instant dislike on first meeting, just as she had instantly warmed to Princess Bagration.

Such ill-natured thoughts made her recollect that the tight and confining stays of her costume were beginning to pinch rather dreadfully, and she decided it might be best to find a quiet and private place where she could undo them slightly. Perhaps it would improve her mood, she thought, gathering up her skirts, wrestling with her farthingale, and making her way through the crowded room.

As she walked down the long arched hallway, dimly lit by the odd brace of candles, she thought that she caught a glimpse of pink-and-white shepherdess dress ahead of her, and a delicate head resting against the strong shoulder of a well-formed man in the national costume of Poland, who could be mistaken for no one else but Prince Adam Czartroyski, for there was not another man in Vienna as handsome and delicately made.

"Oh, Lord," Leonora said aloud, pinching stays forgotten as she feared the worst and hastened her footsteps, hoping to catch up to the amorous couple before any serious damage could be done. How could Jane have been such a fool, she wondered, as to allow even the handsome prince to lure her away to an assignation like this that would ruin her reputation and possibly her life?

The couple seemed to have found an empty room at the end of the corridor, for they turned into it, closing the door.

Leonora quickened her step, feeling her heart pounding in her chest as her hand grasped the gold doorknob, and she turned it, flinging back the door.

Her angry exclamation died away on her lips, and she could only say, "Oh," as she saw that the woman embraced by the handsome prince was not Jane, but Dorothea Talleyrand Périgord, her dark eyes as wide as saucers as she regarded Leonora with surprise and fear.

Leonora could only place her hand over her mouth, murmuring apologies. "I thought you were Jane. Your dress is somewhat similar . . ." she said disjointedly. "Forgive me. I have seen nothing . . ."

Dorothea clung to her lover, who drew himself up to his full height, a protective arm about her waist. "The mistake must have been simple, in the darkness. My dress is very like Jane's. Long ago, when we were both very young, Adam and I met and fell in love. We were to be married, but my mother tore us apart."

"Is it so wrong, madam, to try to snatch a little happiness with the woman you have always loved—will always love?" the prince asked with dignity.

Leonora shook her head. "No, no. I can only wish you both luck and happiness."

Closing the door behind her, she felt a very great fool indeed, and very sad for two people who were so clearly in love, whose lives had been rearranged to suit the whims of others. Let them find their happiness where they could.

Leonora bit her lower lip. Poor Jane, she thought, having felt that ever since Miss Hobart had laid eyes upon the handsome prince, she had been cherishing a *tendre*. How best to tell her that Czartroyski's heart belonged to another lady, and a married lady at that?

She was ruminating rather unhappily upon this subject when an arm, a very masculine arm, seemed to reach out from the darkness of nowhere and grasp her own, dragging her into one of the rooms.

"What—" Leonora gasped in the darkness, quite stunned as the door closed behind her, and she found herself confronted with the hussar Gypsy.

"Well, you damned near blew us all out of the water," Umberto's voice said dryly as he used his firewheel to light a lamp. "I thought you, of all people, would recognize me, Leonora!"

Behind his dark painted face and false mustache, he grinned at her in a most devilish way. "Cat got your tongue? It must be the first time ever."

Leonora put her hands on her hips. "Umberto, what are you doing?" she demanded, and he laid his fingers against her lips.

"Hist! Nothing good, I assure you, so keep your voice low! Thanks to you, the czar has his men looking everywhere for a drunken hussar dressed as a Gyspy. In other words, my dearest Leonora, you have blown my game."

"I don't understand. Why are you going about pretending to be wearing a disguise within a disguise, and why should you care if the czar has his men looking for you? You're not one of his subjects—"

"Ah, but if his bonny boys were to catch me

and search me, they might find something that could prove as hot as hell's hinges for a great many of us, and an embarrassment to the legation." Fumbling in his ragged coat, he produced a velvet box emblazoned with the seal of Russia, tossing it at her casually.

"A czar's dispatch box," she said in wonder.

"Exactly so. It has not been La Bagration's personal charms I have been pursuing these past few weeks," he said, struggling to tear off his false hussar mustache and smear the dark stain from his face. "I told you once that the princess was not above a little espionage herself, recall? She is nearly always in debt, and hoped that those documents would purchase her a little more time with British gold, having purloined it from a certain gentleman's residence in the first place. It's been a great game, with the czar wanting them, and us wanting them back, and now, I fear, it is all over."

There was a pounding on the door. "Lady Leonora! Lady Leonora, are you in there? I must ask you to open the door at once! I have some gentlemen with me who will break it down if you do not!" called Princess Bagration.

Leonora looked at Umberto, stunned. Umberto grinned. "You get them out of here," he said, pressing them into her hands. "As for me, I am behooved to make a quick exit!"

"Lady Leonora!" The door shook on its hinges.

Umberto, quick as a cat, snatched a kiss from Leonora's surprised lips and made his way toward the window. He threw open the sash, swung himself easily over the sill, and was gone.

Leonora, still feeling the taste of his lips on her own, stood for a moment staring after him, and would have rushed to the window to be certain that he did not fall four stories, but the door shook again.

"Lady Leonora! I must see you at once!" the princess called, a note of annoyance creeping into her voice. "I am going to have this door broken down if you do not come out!"

Leonora looked at the small velvet box in her hand for a moment, and then struggled to lift up her heavy velvet skirts. With trembling fingers she worked it securely into the intricate wiring of her farthingale.

"Just a moment, Princess!" she called, as the door, with a heavy crack split from its frame, and two of the czar's footmen, as large as houses, burst through the doorway, followed by the princess, who looked about as if she expected to see another person in the room.

"I was adjusting my hoops," Leonora said, a slight edge on offended modesty in her voice as she smoothed down her velvet skirts. "Certainly nothing that I would want anyone else to witness!" she added with a haughty glance at the footmen, who were stomping about the chamber peering into wardrobes and under chaises.

Princess Bagration was suddenly all smiles again as she fluttered apologetically toward Lady Leonora. "My pardons, dearest friend. But apparently there is a Gypsy thief among us tonight, who used his rags and tatters to sneak in here."

"Oh!" Leonora exclaimed, looking, she hoped, properly horrified. "How dreadful!"

Princess Bagration shivered in her thin costume. "But why do you have the window open on a night as cold as this? You will freeze!"

"I felt a trifle faint, and I thought fresh air would revive me," Leonora said, watching the footmen out of the corner of her eye. If one of them happened to look out and down . . .

"Night air is dangerous," Princess Bagration said solicitously, all charm once again as she took Leonora's arm, gesturing one of the footmen to close the glass. "Come, my dear, what you really need is a glass of champagne. That will revive you better than evil night air could ever do!"

Still talking, she led Leonora down the hallway toward the ball, leaving the two enormous footmen to continue their search.

Caught in the wiring of her skirt, the velvet dispatch box banged against Leonora's hip. "I think I do need a glass of champagne," she admitted quite honestly fanning herself beneath her mask. "This has been a night of so much excitement!" she added fatuously, watching as a short portly gentleman in a red silk domino and a Gypsy costume was discreetly hustled away from the dance floor by more of the czar's footmen.

Doubtless there would be an offended German prince tomorrow, she thought a little headily, lodging a complaint of protocol violation with the czar's people.

She caught sight of Jane, all pink and white, dancing a graceful waltz with a young Roman in a toga, and heaved a sigh, part relief, part sadness, although Jane did not look at all as if she would prefer to be dancing with the prince.

Her hand was claimed by a gentleman in a purple silk domino, and she waltzed out on the dance floor, a little breathless with the idea that she was having an adventure herself.

Would not Catherine Bagration throw a tantrum if she knew that the dispatch box she wanted back so desperately was secure in the hoop skirts of Lady Leonora Ware?

At least Lady Leonora *hoped* it was secure.

It was a relief when Laure Metternich suggested that they take the girls home shortly after the unmasking at midnight. Clearly, things were getting a little more out of hand than either chaperon could have wished, and although the girls sighed and pouted, they both went along willingly enough.

Not so Sir Julian, who was engaged in a flirtation with a haughty Spanish infanta. "What? What? Oh, yes!" he said absently, when Leonora informed him the ladies were leaving. "You go on without me! Yes, yes! And tell Chandler not to wait up!" He winked, a trifle foxed, at Lady Leonora, and she was glad to leave him to his ladies.

They were both yawning when they reached the front door, and Jane declared that she fully intended to sleep until noon, no matter what happened.

It was Chandler himself, rather than one of the Austrian footmen, who opened the door for them. "Lady Leonora," he said in an urgently low voice, "please come in at once. There is someone here for you."

"An assignation?" Jane suggested cheekily, playfully twirling her pink mask.

Chandler drew them into the hall, his face grave. "Your majordomo and I thought it best to leave the other servants out of this, as I am certain you will understand. One may only be a valet, my lady, but one does what one can for England"

"What is going on?" Jane asked, eyes as large as saucers. "Is Papa all right? There has not been an accident?"

"Jane, perhaps you ought to go to bed," Leonora suggested, stripping away her veils and masks and gloves, tossing them carelessly on a chair. "Where is he, Chandler?"

"We took the liberty of placing him in your dressing room, my lady. Miss Strawbridge—a most estimable female!—has staked out your chambers as her territory, and none of the Austrians would dare come near."

"I shall go to him at once," Leonora said, suddenly afraid, picking up her skirts and running up the stairs, with Jane, all curiosity, hot behind her.

Chandler, feeling that he could now place this matter in more competent hands, followed at his usual stately tread.

It was an odd scene that Leonora found in her dressing room. The heavy velvet curtains were tightly drawn, and every lamp that could be found in the upper chambers had been lighted and placed in the room, giving a curious, almost theatrical light to the tableau of René, in his shirtsleeves, and Strawbridge, in her mobcap and dressing gown, bending over the half-naked form of Umberto upon the chaise, a grimace on his rugged features, his darkly stained face pale beneath its disguise, wincing as René dabbed at his shoulder with a red-stained cloth.

"Oh, my God," Jane said, leaning against the doorway, looking quite pale.

"Umberto!" Leonora exclaimed, horrified as she took in the washbasin of pinkish water on the floor and the pile of bloody rags cast carelessly on the rug.

He looked up at her through half-closed eyes, his pupils dark and glittering. "Hullo, Leonora. Told you I would see you again tonight—*damn!*" He winced as René did something to him and held a small black ball up before his eyes.

"The bullet, Lord Umberto," René said calmly enough, although his hands shook a little.

"Now, sir, you'll see that you'll feel more the thing," Strawbridge said, releasing his shoulders from her powerful grip as if extracting bullets from the shoulders of gentlemen were something that she did every day. "I'm sorry, my lady, that I had to tear up some of your petticoats for my lord, but it couldn't be helped. He was bleedin' terrible fierce."

"Wasn't I just," Umberto gasped.

"If you will pardon me for saying so, sir, you are fortunate that you sustained no worse injury. The bullet lodged in your shoulder, rather than passing through and hitting a major organ," Chandler said gravely.

Leonora moved across the room, careful to keep out of the light, and looked down at him, her expression both tender and concerned.

He tried to grin up at her, but it turned into a grimace of pain as René began to apply dressings to his shoulder. He reached for her hand with his own good one, and she gave it to him, feeling how cold it was against her own.

"Did you get away in one piece?" he asked weakly.

"I have it," she assured him, dropping to her knees. "What a perfect little fool I was, Umberto! Forgive me!"

He shook his head, holding tightly to her hand. "Just an adventure, remember?" he asked with a little of his old gaiety. "I worried more about you than me. But I knew that you could take care of yourself, my girl! Up to every rig and row in town!"

"I think, perhaps, Chandler, that a little brandy is called for here," René suggested.

"For Lord Umberto?"

"For all of us!" Jane exclaimed. She had sunk upon a stool in the corner, and having recovered from her initial shock, regarded Lord Umberto with interest. "What did you do? Can you tell us?" she asked.

"I recovered something that belongs to us, and Leonora brought it home for me," he said almost dreamily.

"Well, be that as it may, sir," Strawbridge said, picking up the bloody rags and the bowl of water from the floor, "you keep on havin' these adventures of yours, and there won't be very much left of you to tell about it!"

He grinned at her, and she nodded grimly. Having said her piece, she rustled off, a faint smile on her stern face. "I'll just burn these in the stove, where there won't be any evidence to tell tales to certain snoops in this house."

"An excellent idea, Miss Strawbridge!" Chandler said. "Allow me to assist you!"

René, his bandaging finished, leaned back on his haunches to look at his work. "That will hold you, m'lord. *Mais tiens!*" he shook his head. "Whatever you have done, you have certainly damaged yourself only a little."

"Thank you, René," Umberto said gratefully, moving his shoulder up and down. "Now, if I only had a suit of clothes, I could get back to the legation without any questions being asked."

"I shall see what Chandler can do," René said. "Sir Julian is somewhat your size and build."

"I must say, René, that you are the complete hand!" Umberto grinned.

René pushed a hand through his curls, disarranging his careful pomade. "One does what one can do with what one has, my lord. Do not try to move that shoulder too much, however!"

On his way out the door, he beckoned to Jane. She made a face, and was about to protest that she wanted to stay and hear all about this, when something in René's look gave her face an expression of enlightenment, and she elaborately made a show of following him from the room and closing the door behind her.

"Alone!" Umberto sighed. "You have the box, Lady Leonora?"

Nodding, Leonora rose to her feet and turned her back, pulling up her heavy skirts to work the box loose from the farthingale.

When she presented it to him, he nodded, holding it up to study with his good hand. "Good work, Lady Leonora!" he said approvingly. "Good hiding place, in your hoops!"

She flushed with pleasure. "I . . . well, I almost enjoyed it!" she said. "It was rather fun to have to think very quickly and to intrigue about. I was only afraid for you—"

"With good reason! Someone, probably one of those blasted 'footmen' of the czar's, took a shot at me when I hit the ground." He shook his head. "I must be growing old. There were days in Spain when I relished crawling down the side of a building, from balcony to balcony. No more!"

"Never again?" Leonora asked hopefully.

Umberto laughed, reaching out to stroke her cheek. "Well, perhaps not *ever*," he said softly, and she did not draw away. "My dearest, what have I put you through?"

"It was nothing. Nothing compared to what you must have gone through. But how did you come here?"

"I knew I could not go back to the legation. Too obvious. But no one would think that I would come here, when everyone was out."

Leonora nodded. "And that was what there was all along between you and the princess?"

"That, my dear Leonora, was the sum of the entire thing. One thing, this ought to teach Charlie Stewart to be a little more discreet about where he leaves important papers lying." Umberto shook his head. "I say, that does hurt a bit!" he muttered. "Must be getting old. In the Peninsula I—" He broke off. "You were marvelous," he said simply, taking her hand and kissing it. "No adventuress could have done better, I assure you!"

Leonora smiled, stroking the hair back from Umberto's forehead. "It is not a good thing to have to dance and pretend to be merry when you are worried about someone."

He smiled at her lazily. "If you would do that forever!" he sighed. "Did you really worry about me? You should not, you know!"

"But I do!" Leonora protested.

"And I am glad that you do. It is an interesting feeling, to be worried about by Lady Leonora Ware. After all, she has no heart," Umberto whispered gently, teasing her.

"Perhaps she begins to feel as if there might be one, very tiny, mind you, and only beating very faintly, but still there, nonetheless."

"Whom does it beat for?"

"You know the answer to that," Leonora breathed. "Exasperating, odious, thoroughly charming madman Umberto!"

He laughed, clearly pleased. "And my heart, dearest Leonora. It is hard as a rock, and filled with a geat many crags and cairns, but it beats, and each beat says, 'Leonora,' " he pronounced. "Can you not hear it from there, haughty, fashionable, intriguing wench?"

"I supposed it to be the drip of water in the walls," Leonora laughed. "What fustian you talk, Umberto! You quite make me laugh."

"I would like more, you know, to make you happy," he said thoughtfully. "I doubt that this is the time for this, but damn, I've never done it before! Leonora, will you marry me?"

A shadow crossed her face and she dropped her hand, rising to her feet to pace the room. "If only things were different, yes, I would marry you, Umberto, with all my heart and soul!"

"Then why the devil won't you?" Umberto tried to sit up and dropped back against the chaise with a stifled groan. She crossed the room to him quickly, kneeling at his side. "I'm all right," he said through clenched teeth. "I moved too swiftly for my own good." Reaching out, he grasped her hand into his own, his eyes burning darkly. "Why won't you marry me? I love you, you love me. That is all that we need."

"I cannot marry you, and well you know the reason why," Leonora said desperately. "That duel, six years ago. You killed my husband. Honor would prevent me from every marrying the man who killed my first husband, if nothing else did."

"Honor be damned! Leonora, that was six years ago. If you are worrying about becoming the *on-dit* of London, you are not the female I thought you to be!"

"And what of your career? Such a scandal, dug up again, would not ruin your career?"

"An *old* scandal! Dead and buried. What matters is now, what counts is that we have each other. No one recalls an old scandal."

"But I would always *think!*" Leonora protested.

"How can you dwell in an unhappy past when I offer you a happy future, Leonora?" Umberto asked, genuinely puzzled.

"Oh, please, do not tease me any further. I cannot . . . we cannot! It would always stand between us."

"Not if we did not allow it to do so! Leonora, think of the future, not the past! Think of yourself, of our happiness!"

She shook her head. "I cannot! Oh, I cannot! I want to but I cannot!"

She bounded to her feet and rushed out of the room, her face crimson, her hands pressed to her cheeks.

After the door to her bedroom had closed, two figures emerged from the shadows on the landing below.

Slowly René and Jane drew into the light.

"*C'est terrible, ça,*" René muttered, leaning against the wall and crossing his arms over his chest, a frown on his face. "Is not right, this."

Jane sighed, removing her chipstraw hat. "There they are, the pair of them smelling of April and May since the first moment they laid eyes on each other, and now she won't marry him because of an old scandal that was neither of their faults. René, it is tragic!"

He nodded throughfully. "It is indeed tragic, as you say. Just when we thought he would never come up to scratch, she refuses him!"

"René, there must be something we can do!" Jane said, tugging at his sleeve. "René, you are wonderful at managing, and so am I! If we put our heads together, there must be something we could do!"

"I must think!" René said, cupping his chin in his hand.

Jane looked at him hopefully.

13

IF SHE COULD have done so, Leonora might have slept until Judgment Day, but her dreams were full of Umberto and Princess Bagration, so disturbing that they several times wakened her with a start, only to fall back into a gray slumber again.

It was well past eleven when Strawbridge, a grim look of satisfaction on her face, brought in Leonora's morning tea.

She should have known by Strawbridge's expression that something was amiss, but she was uninterested in anything other than her own misery.

Wordlessly her abigail placed the silver try in her lap. In addition to the tea things, there was a folded piece of paper on the tray, and Leonora eyed Strawbridge for clues as she picked it up and read her own name addressed in a scrawling hand.

My dearest Lady Leonora,

As you must know, for some time René and I have cherished a deep regard for one another.

Now we find that this deep regard has turned to love, love that we know you and Papa would never approve, as René, by birth and breeding an aristocrat, will be impoverished until such time as he regains his lands and position.

So we have eloped, and will return to Paris, where we hope that Louis will restore his family lands and titles. Then I shall be a countess and Papa cannot object. Please forgive me.

I am, ma'am, ever your,
Jane Hobart

"Good God!" Leonora said, all thoughts of her own problems suddenly driven from her head as she read this epistle a second time, finding it even worse than the first.

"Strawbridge!" she exclaimed, knocking over the tray as she got out of bed. "Where is Sir Julian? You must find him at once!"

"He didn't come in at all last night, my lady," Strawbridge said grimly. "And who's to say where he might be this morning?"

"Well, you must send a footman to the legation at once! And have René—oh, damn!— René, Strawbridge, has run off with Miss Hobart!"

Strawbridge's lips set in a thin line. "I would have expected as much, my lady, to see the pair of them lately. Shall I get Chandler, ma'am?"

"Oh, I know not what to do or whom to summon! René used to do all of that for me!"

Leonora exclaimed, distractedly pulling a comb through her hair.

"My lord Umberto is still asleep in the dressing room, my lady," Strawbridge remarked. "Now, iffen I say so, he's the man that would know what to do next."

"Does Jane understand what she is doing?" Leonora asked herself anxiously, pulling on her dressing gown. "Do either of them understand what they are doing? One always thought René preferred . . ." Distraught, she rubbed her aching temples with her fingers. "If only Sir Julian were here! This should be his problem, after all! Hang that man!"

Knotting the cord, she tried the knob of the connecting door, rather stunned to find it locked, as if Umberto suspected she might have designs on his virtue during the evening.

"Umberto!" she cried, pounding on the door.

In a second, it was opened by the unflappable Chandler. "Good morning, my lady," he intoned. "Lord Umberto is dressing, so if you would be good enough to—"

"Oh, hang Umberto!" Lady Leonora said, stepping past the elderly valet to find Umberto bathed and in his shirtsleeves, his arms half in his coat. "Ah, good morning, Leonora," Umberto said with more warmth than she felt she had any right to expect.

"*Please* allow me to do that, sir," Chandler said reproachfully. "With your arm, such movements are most painful to execute." He resumed delicately fitting Umberto in his black jacket.

"You must read this at once!" Leonora cried, thrusting the letter at Umberto. "The worst possible thing has happened!"

Wincing as Chandler fitted him, Umberto shook his head. "Have to read it to me! Although what it could be to bring you dashing in here in that very fetching dressing gown . . ."

Unfolding the note at eye level, Leonora effectively silenced Umberto. If that perfect gentleman's gentleman, Chandler, just happened to read it over Umberto's shoulder, he could not be faulted.

Umberto's expression changed from that of busy cheer to genuine concern by the time he was at the bottom of the page, moving his head impatiently as Chandler sought to tie his cravat.

"But I always thought René—" he said.

"Myself also! But there you have it! Why, it must have been going on for weeks, and none of us noticed! Umberto, please, what am I to do?" Leonora begged.

His jaw hardened. "Send for Sir Julian. *His* problem, after all."

"Pardon me, sir, but Sir Julian did not come in last night." Chandler coughed delicately. "Such is sometimes his custom, sir," he added.

"So I am given to understand," Leonora said. "I've sent a footman round to the legation—"

Umberto shook his head, doing up his cuffs. "Could take hours to track him down. No telling where a man might be at this time of day."

"But there's no time to waste!" Leonora

exclaimed, clasping her hands together. "Oh, please, Umberto! I do so need you!"

He looked up at her, one eyebrow raised slightly, and she regarded him with wide eyes.

"I took the liberty, sir, of having your chaise brought around while you dressed," Chandler told the ceiling.

"Go and dress yourself, Lady Leonora, in an outfit suitable for catching runaway lovers. They can only have taken the road to Linz."

In a daze, Leonora retreated to her own room, where Strawbridge already had her carriage dress laid out.

In fifteen minutes' time, she joined Umberto, in his sixteen-caped driving coat, pacing the hallway.

"Let us go," he said gruffly, handing her up into the chaise and dismissing his groom.

They drove out of the city at a spanking pace behind a lively team of matched bays.

"I suppose you should have every reason to be angry with me after last night," Leonora said rather meekly, her hands folded in her lap.

"Perhaps I expected too much. I am not much used to courting women. In fact, you are the first lady I have ever proposed to!" Umberto's jaw twitched, but he did not remove his eyes from the road. "To say that I was disappointed would be truthful, would it not?"

"Pray do not be angry with me right now! I could not bear it, not on top of this!" Leonora pleaded anxiously. "Oh, none of this would have ever happened if I had never come to this *stoopid* Congress!"

"You see what comes of having no heart," Umberto said. "You end up chasing eloping lovers across the countryside!"

They rode along in silence for the space of an hour, when Umberto drew up on the reins. "Hullo—what's this?" he demanded.

A charming half-timbered inn, nestled among the autumn fields, sat slightly back from the road. Leaning across Umberto, Leonora saw Sir Julian's barouche in the yard.

"I think we have found them!" Leonora exclaimed.

Lord Umberto brought his team into the yard at a spanking pace, throwing the reigns to an ostler and jumping down from the perch with a grimace. "You may wait here!" he ordered Leonora abruptly.

"I shall not!" she replied spunkily, and trailed behind him into the inn.

Peering into the parlor, they were stopped short in their tracks as they both saw René, his curls perfect, his bottle-green waistcoat gleaming from the light of a neatly laid fire as he supervised a waiter in the laying of the table.

His boots struck the floor as Umberto strode into the room. "René, my good man! A word with you if you please!"

René looked up, and rather than the horror they expected, a broad smile broke out across his face. "Ah, Lady Leonora, Lord Umberto! Just in time, I see!" he exclaimed.

"René!" Leonora demanded. "Where is Jane? What have you done with her?"

"Done with her?" René looked puzzled. "I

should suppose that right now she is enjoying her tea with Countess Zichy, as she rose up this morning and was called for by that lady in her carriage. I believe that the plan was for a group of young ladies and their beaux and gallants to ride out of town, eat an *al fresco* luncheon by some scenic site, and return in time for supper."

"You mean she's not here?" Leonora asked, puzzled.

René shook his curls. "*Mais, non,* my lady. But I have been here since this morning making everything ready, as you can see."

"Damn, René! What the devil does this all mean?" Umberto demanded dangerously. "I ought to draw your cork!"

René held up his hands in protest. "I would rather that you did not," he said. "Have a glass of merlot instead. Austrian wines are quite interesting, I think."

In spite of themselves, they accepted a glass of wine each from René, while he gave them his most charming smile.

"Now, what is this all about? I received a note this morning from Jane saying that you and she had eloped—"

"Ah, Lady Leonora, that was a mere ruse, I fear. You see, Jane and I put our heads together and decided that this had been going on long enough. When it is clear to everyone in the world but you that my lord and my lady were created *par le bon Dieu* for each other, than it is time for others to step in and take a hand. One could not help but be outside the door listening last night when my lord finally came to scratch and my lady refused for reasons that would not fill a thimble! So we have decided that you will never come to your senses and marry unless we help you along a little!"

"Marry?" Umberto said blankly.

"Marry?" Leonora repeated.

"Marry!" René said triumphantly. "To this end, I have even found a minister, a vicar traveling through Austria with two students in his charge, who has agreed to perform the ceremony at six o'clock tonight, after he returns from his tour of the Hofburg. So that is how we contrive to bring you together! A good meal waits, good wines, a very nice bedroom upstairs with a beautiful vista out across the fields and hedgerows. In short, the elopment is yours, not that of Jane and me!"

"I don't believe this!" Umberto said, seating himself heavily.

"I do," Leonora laughed. "Only you and Jane would ever think of such a scheme! To make us drive all the way out here together, only to find that it's our wedding you propose, not your own . . ."

René nodded understandingly. "And Miss Strawbridge has packed your portmanteau. It is in your room. Lord Umberto, I took a liberty in packing yours, but I think you will find all is in order. My lady, I have laid out your pomona-green silk. Most suitable, I think, for a second wedding."

With a bow, he retreated from the room, completely self-satisfied.

"Do we seem to have a choice in this matter?" Umberto asked, incredulous.

"I think not!" Leonora laughed, shaking her head. "Only think how disappointed they would be if we were to return tonight, unmarried!"

"Does this mean that you actually are considering marrying me?" Umberto asked, enveloping Leonora most securely into his driving cape.

She nodded. "I want a happy future, Umberto! I can no longer live in the past. Piffle to old scandals! We shall create a few new ones ourselves!"

Slowly, and with his sardonic smile, he bent to kiss her upturned lips. "Starting now," he murmured devilishly.

About the Author

CAROLINE BROOKS is a practising gerentologist who resides in Rising Sun, Maryland, with her husband and three children. Her interest in the Regency period was sparked when she purchased an old diary from that era in a Charing Cross bookstall during a visit to London in her student days.

SIGNET Regency Romances You'll Want to Read

(0451)

☐ THE REPENTANT REBEL by Jane Ashford. (131959—$2.50)*
☑ THE IMPETUOUS HEIRESS by Jane Ashford. (129687—$2.25)*
☐ FIRST SEASON by Jane Ashford. (126785—$2.25)*
☐ A RADICAL ARRANGEMENT by Jane Ashford. (125150—$2.25)*
☐ THE HEADSTRONG WARD by Jane Ashford. (122674—$2.25)*
☐ THE MARCHINGTON SCANDAL by Jane Ashford. (116232—$2.25)*
☐ THE THREE GRACES by Jane Ashford. (114183—$2.25)*
☐ A COMMERCIAL ENTERPRISE by Sandra Heath. (131614—$2.50)*
☐ MY LADY DOMINO by Sandra Heath. (126149—$2.25)*
☑ THE MAKESHIFT MARRIAGE by Sandra Heath. (122682—$2.25)*
☐ MALLY by Sandra Heath. (093429—$1.75)*
☐ THE OPERA DANCER by Sandra Heath. (111125—$2.25)*
☐ THE UNWILLING HEIRESS by Sandra Heath. (097718—$1.95)*
☐ MANNERBY'S LADY by Sandra Heath. (097726—$1.95)*
☑ THE SHERBORNE SAPPHIRES by Sandra Heath. (097718—$1.95)*
☑ THE CLERGYMAN'S DAUGHTER by Julia Jefferies. (120094—$2.25)*
☐ THE CHADWICK RING by Julia Jefferies. (113462—$2.25)*

*Prices slightly higher in Canada.

**Buy them at your local
bookstore or use coupon
on next page for ordering.**

Other Regency Romances from SIGNET

(0451)

☑ THE INCORRIGIBLE RAKE by Sheila Walsh. (131940—$2.50)*
☑ THE DIAMOND WATERFALL by Sheila Walsh. (128753—$2.25)*
☑ A SUITABLE MATCH by Sheila Walsh. (117735—$2.25)*
☑ THE RUNAWAY BRIDE by Sheila Walsh. (125142—$2.25)*
☑ A HIGHLY RESPECTABLE MARRIAGE by Sheila Walsh. (118308—$2.25)*
☑ THE INCOMPARABLE MISS BRADY by Sheila Walsh. (092457—$1.75)*
☑ THE ROSE DOMINO by Sheila Walsh. (110773—$2.25)*
☐ THE AMERICAN BRIDE by Megan Daniel. (124812—$2.25)*
☐ THE UNLIKELY RIVALS by Megan Daniel. (110765—$2.25)*
☐ THE SENSIBLE COURTSHIP by Megan Daniel. (117395—$2.25)*
☐ THE RELUCTANT SUITOR by Megan Daniel. (096711—$1.95)*
☐ AMELIA by Megan Daniel. (094875—$1.75)*

*Prices slightly higher in Canada

Buy them at your local bookstore or use this convenient coupon for ordering.

NEW AMERICAN LIBRARY,
P.O. Box 999, Bergenfield, New Jersey 07621

Please send me the books I have checked above. I am enclosing $_____
(please add $1.00 to this order to cover postage and handling). Send check
or money order—no cash or C.O.D.'s. Prices and numbers are subject to change
without notice.

Name _____

Address_____

City_____ State_____ Zip Code_____
Allow 4-6 weeks for delivery.
This offer is subject to withdrawal without notice.